Paint Me Yours

Rachel Bowdler

Content Warnings

Mentions of drug and alcohol addiction

Discussions of weight and fatphobia

Strained familial relationships

One

There was no way of identifying Greystone Gallery from the outside. Eliza had wandered past it four times before realising that the narrow little building sandwiched between a crumbling cottage and a charity shop was, in fact, the place she had spent the last half an hour searching for.

That left her running very late — and Eliza did not like running late.

With an irritated huff, she smoothed down her blazer before inviting herself in. The fine coat of grey paint covering the door was chipped and faded, and from that alone, Eliza knew she would have her work cut out for her here.

The interior only confirmed it. There was no structure to the way the art had been exhibited. Paintings and photography smattered the walls seemingly at random, each with a different frame. Black. White. Wood. Rose gold. A black and white street landscape had been hung beside a colourful, abstract acrylic painting. A minimalistic sketch beside a vibrant portrait of a ginger tabby cat.

Eliza examined the wall closest, muttering her disapproval under her breath. "Oh, dear. What sort of gallery are you running here, Benny?"

"I believe it's usually categorised as an *art* gallery," a rough voice quipped far too close to Eliza's ear.

Startled, she whipped around... and faltered. She had not seen Benny in almost a decade, and were it not for those slitted, brown eyes — lined faintly now with what was surely eyeliner — and the lopsided smirk, she would not have recognised him at all. When her mother had told her that Benny had strayed from his family's pristine image, she had not been exaggerating. He was all mussed, shaggy hair that fell to his jaw, trimmed beard shadowing his chin. And his arms...

His arms were covered in tattoos she doubted Henry Weatherford would approve of. He was not even *dressed* as a respectable gallery owner with his red shirt unbuttoned to his chest and slouchy, frayed denim jeans hanging off his hips. Eliza could not help but take the transformation in with an arched eyebrow. He had been such a clean and chiselled twenty-year-old, the epitome of the Weatherford class and elegance. What had happened in the last thirteen years to cause such a dramatic change?

"Is there a problem, Miss...?" He trailed off expectantly.

He didn't recognise her, either. Why did that make her stomach twist unpleasantly? It wasn't as though they had ever been that close. And it *had* been ten years. They had both changed — her more than him, it seemed, if he didn't know her anymore.

"Braybrooke," she responded, words clipped. "Eliza Braybrooke."

Benny's mouth parted in surprise. He at least recognised her by name, then. "Right. Eliza. Bloody hell. I didn't recognise you."

"It's been a long time." She rocked on her heels uncomfortably as he scoured her from head to toe. Searching for some old remnant of the Eliza he remembered, perhaps, just as she was with him.

"Well, it's... it's good to see you," he sputtered out with a soft chuckle. "What brings you here?"

It only occurred to her then that Henry hadn't warned Benny to expect Eliza. It left her unsettled, but she pushed that weight down before she could overthink it. "I'm here on behalf of your father. He hired me to curate the gallery. Revamp it, if you will."

At the mention of Henry, Benny's once warm features drained of colour. "I don't need a curator, and I definitely don't need a revamp."

"I beg to differ," Eliza said lightly, scanning the exhibits again with more than a little distaste. "The place is a little... disorganised."

"The place is *mine*," Benny bit back, voice lowering with a venom she hadn't been expecting. "I like it how it is."

Eliza pursed her lips and eyed his rugged appearance again. He looked as though he had been dragged through a hedge of thorns and branches — backwards. "I imagine you do."

"Meaning?"

Sucking in a breath, Eliza wandered to the next piece. A monochrome splattering of black ink on coffee-stained parchment paper. She had spent three years studying all sorts of art and could not even begin to understand what this one meant; what purpose it served. "Just that you certainly have unique taste."

Benny followed behind, a looming shadow, and Eliza repressed a shudder at the feeling of him so close. Too close. As though he was trying to shepherd her out. "It sounds like my father, sending somebody all the way to my gallery just to patronise me."

"Except it's not your gallery, is it?" Eliza crossed her arms over her chest, stiff blazer pulling across her back as she stared Benny down. A curiosity she refused to yield to niggled just below the surface of her. She had no idea what Benny's relationship was like with his father these days, though she recalled it had always been strained — and the fact that she had not seen Benny return to Torquay for Henry's dinner parties or summer soirées spoke volumes. Even Declan, Benny's brother, never mentioned him in conversation. "Your father owns everything. That means he has a right to hire whomever he wishes to change it as he sees fit. That's why I'm here."

Benny's face flushed a petulant red. "He's never even come near this gallery before. Why does he want to be involved now?"

Eliza shrugged. "I suppose he's concerned that his investment isn't performing well. I can't imagine why."

"My answer is no."

"You seem to be under the impression that you have a choice." Eliza's voice turned frosty, and she narrowed her eyes at the man in front of her. He was such a painful cliché: the rebellious rich boy who let his father pay for everything but still complained at any chance he got. "You don't. Mr. Weatherford wishes for me to curate *his* gallery. I will. Whether you want to be involved in the process or not is your call."

"*Nothing* in this gallery is changing. I'll talk to my father and sort this out myself. Sorry for the wasted trip, but your services are not needed here."

Eliza couldn't help but roll her eyes as she dug out a pamphlet from her purse and thrust it into Benny's hands. He didn't take it, so she pressed it flat against his chest, leaving him to stumble back slightly.

"Talk to your father. I have no doubt he'll give you the same answer I have. This place is... Well, it's a mess, Benny. The fact there's not another soul in here only proves it. Nobody is going to want to see or buy art like this." She gestured to the ink splatter to prove her point. "And when you come to see sense, if you still doubt me, my most recent exhibit opens on Saturday. You can see for yourself how I work."

"And then what?" Benny's upper lip curled in contempt — so different from the warm smile he had offered only a few minutes ago. "You'll replace all of my local artists with pretentious ones that my customers will never be able to afford? My work is on these walls. My *friends'* work is on these walls. They're not going anywhere."

"And they don't have to." Eliza forced herself not to search for Benny's work out of sheer curiosity. She hoped to God that it wasn't the one she had just criticised in front of him. "You can keep a section for local artists. But you need more than just a random collection of work, Benny. Right now, it isn't an exhibit. It's a replica of a children's sketchbook."

"And I suppose they taught you all that at Oxford, did they?"

"Cambridge," she corrected, scowling at the judgement fringing his tone. "And yes. As a matter of fact, they did. Where did you get your art education, Benny?"

"Nowhere you'd like, I'd imagine," he hissed, and he seemed more than just unhappy, now; he seemed livid. Why hadn't Henry prepared her for this? She was used to difficult clients, but Benny... Benny looked like he wanted to put her head through a canvas. "I don't remember you being this snooty."

"I don't remember you being this bratty," she retorted, placing her hands on her hips and glowering. "Believe it or not, I'm trying to help you."

"You're trying to help my father. That's the opposite of helping me."

Eliza scoffed. "I'm not here to get caught in the middle of your petty little feud. I'm here to do my job. Whether you like it or not, I'm staying."

"We'll see."

She schooled herself to remain calm, taking a step back to put some distance between them. She hadn't even noticed how close they'd been standing until she'd caught a whiff of musky cologne.

"Talk to your father," she advised steadily. "And then get back to me."

"Don't hold your breath."

Eliza only jeered at Benny a final time before marching out of the gallery. As soon as the door had slammed shut behind her, she cursed the bastard out under her breath, sending a final glare through the gallery's window as she made her way back to her car.

The sooner she got out of St. Agnes and away from Benny Weatherford, the better.

Benny punched his father's number into his phone as soon as Eliza left, chest heaving with a rage he had spent years learning to keep in check. All it had taken was one conversation to go back to that awful, all-consuming place where everything burned and his gut writhed, and he just wanted it to *stop*.

But he wouldn't let Henry Weatherford destroy everything he had built here. He wouldn't let anybody touch his gallery. It was the only thing he had. So, he waited while the phone dialled, swallowing down deep breaths. His free hand curled tightly into a fist, chewed nails leaving angry crescent moons etched into his palms.

His father picked up after five rings. "Henry Weatherford."

The nasally voice reminded Benny of nails against a chalkboard, setting his teeth on edge.

"What do you want with the gallery?" He growled, too furious to waste any time on forced greetings and small talk. His father was not one for niceties, anyway. Not with Benny, at least. They had long since stopped pretending otherwise.

"I suppose Miss Braybrooke informed you of my plans to freshen up the place."

"There's nothing to freshen. I won't be needing her assistance."

"Since I'm investing my money into the property and the business, I'll be the judge of that." Henry's voice remained terse, as though Benny was a business associate rather than his son. Nothing had changed, then. "And since I haven't seen any sort of profit or repayment yet, your options are limited. I can sell the place if you'd rather."

The thought of losing the gallery left ice pooling in Benny's gut. It was all he had. Without it... He didn't want to think of where that would leave him.

"You've never paid an interest in it before," was all he could choke out. "This is the only thing I've ever asked of you."

"The *only* thing?" Henry repeated, voice rising in disbelief. "I spend a substantial amount to keep your little money pit afloat. I haven't seen a penny of any of it returned. And I'm sure I don't need to remind you of the other things I've paid for on your behalf over the years."

Of course. Of course Henry would hold those things over his head, though Benny knew the gallery barely made a dent in his funds. He had been trying his best since he'd bought the place to earn enough to pay his father back, but commissioning artists wasn't cheap and he rarely had any buyers to even out the expenditures. He'd come to St Agnes without a penny. Sometimes, he wished he had never asked his father for help. He'd be better off on the streets than having this conversation with him now.

Raking his mussed hair back, Benny sighed. "I intend to pay you back."

"I'm sure you do. When pigs fly, perhaps."

He ground his teeth together, nails digging harder still into the clammy flesh of his fist. "So this is it, then? You're having one of your minions take over my gallery so that you can get your money back?"

"Don't be so dramatic, Benjamin. Miss Braybrooke's job is merely to source new artists and better the gallery's exhibitions. Is it honestly so terrible that I want to improve your business?"

Yes. Anything with his father ended up terrible. But if he kept arguing, he'd only go round in circles. Still, Henry's reasoning didn't sit right. He had never cared about the gallery before; had pretended, in fact, that it hadn't existed at all for the past three years, and Benny had preferred it that way.

"Okay." Benny braced himself against his desk, squeezing his eyes shut until the last dregs of fury left him. "If the gallery brings in enough profit that my debts are repaid, will that make us even? Will you sign the gallery over to me?"

The line fell silent. Benny imagined his father sitting at a fancy, glossy desk in his office, ankle crossed over his thigh as the greedy cogs in his head turned the offer around.

"If the gallery becomes a worthwhile investment with Miss Braybrooke's help, then yes," Henry agreed finally. "The gallery will be yours when you can afford it."

"Then you and I will be done. No more holding it all over my head."

"Would I do such a thing?" scoffed Henry.

It was reason enough for Benny to give in. He needed this gallery. He needed this chance at independence. "Alright. Fine."

"Good. I'll check in in a few weeks to see how my new employee is faring."

"Can't wait."

Benny hung up and let the tension fall away. He didn't want

this. He loved the gallery; loved what it did for others as well as himself. But he hated his father, and if Eliza could solve his problems, make the gallery more successful, he would try if only to crawl out from under Henry's thumb once and for all.

The pamphlet that Eliza had given him earlier still lay on the desk. He browsed it with little interest, supposing that if he was to agree to this, he at least needed to gauge how Eliza would work in his space.

A wave of dread rolled through him at the sight of such grand exhibitions, but he would not crumble beneath it. Eliza might have plans for his gallery, but he would not let her take everything he had built. If they were doing this, they would do it on his terms.

He would tell her so when he visited her exhibit on Saturday.

Two

Benny had to suffer through two hours of weekend traffic to get to the exhibit in Exeter. It was held in a grand museum towering across the city with its jagged, Gothic architecture — and from what he could tell, it was a success thus far.

He supposed he could see why.

The gallery had been laid out into sections spanning chronologically, starting with old impressionist oil paintings he vaguely recognised to modern-day fine art by up and coming British artists. It was like travelling through time — and not as conventional and snobby as Benny had expected either. A lot of the artwork came from marginalised painters and sculptors rather than the classics. No Monet or Picasso in sight.

But it wasn't him. Eliza might have known her art history, and she might have spent an enormous amount of time curating for the huge exhibit, but what good would she be in an independent little gallery in St Agnes that prided itself in displaying local talent?

By lunch time, the place brimmed with families. Kids ran riot through the arched thresholds and glossy floors, uninterested in anything but the gift shop and the cakes being sold in the small cafe in the corner. He watched as others — snobby, rich people, he'd wager from the way they dressed and held themselves — turned their nose up at them, spending an excruciatingly, unnecessary amount of time analysing each painting. There were few that Benny lingered on for longer than a moment or two. In the end, the one he couldn't quite leave behind was a landscape of a marina that reminded him an awful lot of the place he'd grown up in. The sun-bleached docks and tall boat masts piercing clear sky did not bring warm memories of childhood. They only re-

minded him of how lonely he had been in Torquay, watching the
tethered yachts bob on the grey sea. He remembered feeling like
one of those boats — the rusted, abandoned ones that nobody used
anymore: tied down, carried along but never really moving, a little
bit worn and grotty and forgotten.

"Well, well, well." The familiar drawl behind him broke
Benny from his trance. Dread plummeted through his stomach as
he turned, finding his brother smirking. "If it isn't my long lost big
brother."

'Long lost' was a tad dramatic, though it was true that
Benny hadn't seen Declan in years. It seemed that luck had come
to an end now. Both Weatherfords in one week was slightly more
than he could handle.

"Dec," Benny nodded soberly, "I wasn't expecting to see you
at a museum. Have you finally decided to crawl out of Dad's arse?"

It was no secret that despite Henry's investment in the gallery, given mostly so that he could maintain control over his poor,
stray son, the Weatherfords had no interest in art — not unless it
brought the money in, at least. The first time that Benny had told
his father he wanted to be an artist, shortly before he left home,
Henry had laughed in his face and handed him a pile of prospec-
tuses for business schools instead.

"Funny." Declan snorted. "Have *you* finally decided to crawl
out of that ramshackle little cave you hide out in while leeching off
his money?"

"If I'd have known you were coming, I would have stayed
there." Benny flashed his teeth with a grin that dripped with nothing but scorn. He hated his brother. He hated that Declan was
just like his father, and that he'd always used their alliance to tear
down Benny. He hated that it hadn't always been that way, not
until Declan had let himself be poisoned.

"He tells me he hired Eliza to revamp the place. Still getting
other people to fix your messes, I see."

Benny had no response to that; nothing but the acid that
roiled in his stomach, made flesh in the way he bristled.

"And here she is now," Declan continued, dark eyes glittering as they shifted past Benny, to something — someone — behind him. "The woman of the hour."

Eliza sidled up beside Declan with more than a little wariness, offering Benny a terse smile as Declan snaked a hand around her waist.

Oh, God. No. Was Eliza dating his brother as well as working for his father? What, exactly, was he agreeing to in letting her into the gallery?

"I'm glad you came, Benny." Her melodic voice was friendly enough — not as it had been in the gallery a few days ago. Still, she wasn't the girl he remembered.

Benny's first real memory of Eliza was one from the day they'd met. Benny had been a reserved ten-year-old with none of the etiquette his father had tried to engrain in him — but Eliza... Eliza had bumbled down the garden steps in the midday sun, asking to play hide and seek while her parents ate lunch with his father on the patio. He remembered how she'd stopped and gasped when she'd reached the grass, pointing at the array of daisies and buttercups littering the lawn. He'd frozen completely when Eliza plucked the latter from the ground and held it to his throat, the petals tickling the faint beginnings of his Adam's apple; had only been able to shudder against the soft flutter on such a sensitive patch of skin as she'd asked him if he liked butter and then giggled.

It was the first time he had known tenderness. Since his mother's death two years before, his life had been spent thrust between sharp-edged adults always throwing barbed criticisms his way. Eliza had been the opposite. A soft, giggling little girl who only wanted to know if a stranger liked butter, and had been curious enough to force a flower beneath his chin for the answer. A reprieve.

He hadn't liked it, either — not until she'd told him excitedly that his throat reflected the bright yellow, and that meant he loved butter. After that, he'd started to ask for it on his sandwiches, thinking of that moment each time he ate.

But that was a long, long time ago, and they had never been as close as that initial meeting again. Declan had been closer to her in age, and he had charmed her easily with the manners and arrogance his father had taught him well into their teens. It seemed that, at least, had not changed.

Benny nodded now, trying to gather his composure enough to respond; trying to stop looking for that piece of her, and the piece of him who had been drawn to her so strongly. They were not those children anymore. "We got off to a bad start. I'm sorry for that."

"Benny gets off to a bad start with everyone," Declan taunted.

Benny was sure he didn't imagine the way that Eliza leaned further away from his brother's embrace in response. Good. It wasn't true. Not anymore, anyway. He was better now.

He tried to remind himself of that as he forced a strained smile. "Would you perhaps give us a moment to discuss business, Dec?"

Declan's steely, brown eyes snagged between Benny and Eliza, but it was Eliza who gave him an encouraging nod. He managed to fit in a final sneer towards Benny before he dawdled off with his hands in his pockets, paying no heed to the art around him.

"You're still close with my brother, I see." A familiar, cold hand fisted his gut, as though he was still that ten-year-old who didn't fit in. He hated himself for it.

Eliza shrugged, pale eyes flitting to the artwork he'd been admiring before the interruption. "Do you like this one?"

"It's Torquay Harbour, isn't it?"

"It is. That's not an answer, though."

"It brings back a lot of memories I'd rather forget," he admitted, chewing on his lip before he turned away from the painting.

"Still not an answer." Eliza's pink-painted lips curled with the beginnings of a smirk. She gestured towards the next section. "Have you visited the planetarium upstairs yet?"

"I thought I was here for your work." That light teasing flickered in his own voice now, too, as though she'd infected him with it. It surprised even him.

"My work can never compete with the stars," she murmured wistfully — and it was her again. The seven-year-old clutching a buttercup in her hand, all tenderness and warmth. They began to wander away from the main exhibits. "But I assume you're here because you've realised just how badly you need me."

Benny released a throaty chuff at that. "Someone thinks highly of themselves."

"Well, it is my exhibit you're standing in, is it not?" She grinned and led him up the stairs, where — God help him — even more children screamed and played. The walls were covered in constellations and tidbits of information about astrology, leading into a domed planetarium. A lulling voice doing its best to imitate David Attenborough's drifted through the speakers with tales of the Milky Way as twinkling, computer-generated starlight flitted across the floor.

"For the record," she muttered over the droning narrator, "I apologise for my behaviour, too. I didn't know your relationship with your father was so… frayed. Though I suppose I should have guessed, since I haven't seen you in the same room for a good decade."

"It's complicated," he brushed off with a voice that was steadier than he felt. The last thing he'd expected from her was an apology. "I'm agreeing to this under two conditions."

"Here we go." Eliza rolled her eyes, but the humour still danced on her lips. She was more beautiful than he remembered her being — in the elegant, wealthy sort of way his own family were. He supposed that was why Declan still held an interest in her.

"One." He counted on his ringed finger, light bouncing off the silver bands he'd collected from charity shops and market stalls. "I get the final say in any changes you make. Any new art needs my approval first. If we do this, you and I are going to have to cooperate."

"My primary concern is making sure my clients are happy," Eliza replied, leaning against the railings that separated them from the star-speckled screens. "However, that means that *you* have to trust my judgement, too. Nothing will change if you don't let me change it."

"We'll see," Benny dismissed. "And don't interrupt my conditions. I practiced them this morning."

Amusement danced across her features. "Go ahead."

"Two." A second finger. "The artists remain local to St Agnes, or at least within the South West. My intention has always been to showcase people who struggle to get their work seen. That won't change in favour of whatever snotty —"

"Pretentious artists you think I favour," she finished for him with a sigh. "Fine. I get it. I agree."

"I should probably also make it clear that I'm only accepting your help to get my father off my back. Whatever changes come of this are for the good of the gallery. If I generate enough profit, Henry has agreed to hand it over to me for good, so if we're going to do this, we do it properly."

"And here I was thinking you just wanted me around." Something indecipherable flickered across her features. "Okay. You have a deal. Just do me a favour and get a few more lights in that place. Nobody is going to buy art if they can't see it."

Benny shook his head, already regretting his decision. "One second in and you're already making demands."

Eliza only smiled — a dazzling, confident smile that made her rosy cheeks swell. "It's what I do. Get used to it."

Three

Benny looked less than happy about Eliza's early arrival on Monday morning. He stayed out of her way, sipping coffee and sketching behind the front desk while she rearranged the artwork on display, choosing her favourites for the front exhibit and window displays.

By lunch time, half of the walls were empty, the other half organised by their medium. "Alright." She dusted off her hands and took a step back from her work, back aching from being on her feet for so long. "I've chosen my personal favourites and set them up at the front. What do you think?"

Benny abandoned his drawing, rounding the counter with his features pressed into a thin line. As he settled beside her to examine the wall, his cologne curled around her again — musky and fringed with spice. She tried not to think of how close those tattooed arms were to her own.

She could not deny that she found him attractive, even if he did look like he needed a good haircut and a shave. He was everything that Declan was not: rugged and worn as old boots. And though Eliza did not want to, she still remembered the painful crush she had harboured for him in her late teens, before Benny had strayed from the Weatherfords for good. Whatever had conspired since had clearly roughed him up. And yet beneath the scruffy beard and loose clothes, those brown eyes were as warm as she remembered — only more haunted now. More experienced. They still had that same sharp, tingly effect on her sometimes, as though capable of dragging up feelings buried long ago.

That didn't mean to say she didn't still find him incredibly irritating. Even the smirk that curled crookedly across his lips as he took in the photography section set her teeth on edge.

"These are your favourites?"

"I think they're the ones that will generate the most attention and interest, yes." She set her jaw in defiance, cocking her head to glare at him. "Why? Is there a problem with them?"

"No problem," Benny drawled. "I'm just flattered that you're such a big fan of my work."

Eliza frowned in confusion, and then understood a moment later, when Benny pointed to the signature in the corner of one of the photographs. BW. Benny Weatherford. She had chosen a few with that same, zigzagging scribble on the bottom: a portrait of an elderly woman named Vera that warred with shadows and light; a landscape of a lighthouse beaming onto a black ocean; a macro of seafoam washing onto the beach, curling between chipped shells and pebbles. All of them had been edited in black and white, and Eliza admired the choice. It drew attention to the most mundane of details and made them beautiful.

In fact, she had thought these ones were the best work in the gallery.

She blushed with that knowledge now, crossing her arms over her chest with as much nonchalance as she could muster. "Don't get too cocky. You don't have much other photography to contend with here."

"Most photographers sell their own prints." He shrugged.

"Why don't you?" Other than the framed pieces, she saw no other print styles on show. Most photographers sold postcards or posters of their work, or even T-shirts and canvas bags. Benny had none of that.

"There would be no point wasting my money on something that wouldn't generate profit."

Eliza frowned. Benny had jested, but his words, said without any emotion whatsoever, implied he didn't realise just how good his work was. "What makes you think it won't generate profit? People like to buy prints. They're cheaper and more versatile than paintings."

"But as you so politely put it, nobody wants to buy art like this." He opened his arms to the empty space to prove his point.

"Look around. Have you seen one customer come in this morning? I don't even have people browsing anymore."

Indeed, Eliza had been able to work uninterrupted this morning. Nobody had entered save for her. "Well, perhaps it would help if it was clear from the outside that this place is a gallery," she reasoned. "It took me half an hour to find it last week. It looks just like any other apartment building. You need a sign outside."

"And I suppose I'll pay for that with the money tree I grow in the backyard."

Eliza huffed in frustration, arms slapping to her sides. Stubborn. He was so bloody stubborn. "To make a business successful, Benny, you have to invest in it. You can't just hang a bunch of mediocre pieces in here and hope that somebody wanders in. Why don't you ask your father —"

"No. My father is staying as far away from the gallery as I can keep him."

"And how's that working for you?" she retorted, arching her eyebrow. "Last time I checked, he pays for almost everything here, including me."

"No," Benny hissed again, a muscle in his jaw ticking. "I won't ask him for more money."

"You're asking him for an investment that will end up benefiting him in the long run. What is this whole feud with your father about, anyway? What happened between the two of you?"

Features shuttering, Benny marched back to his desk, beginning to scribble in his sketchbook again with a black biro as though he had not heard Eliza at all. Still, she saw the telltale signs of suppressed anger twitching in his neck and the squaring of his shoulders.

Eliza huffed in defeat. "I have a meeting with your father tomorrow after I visit another artist's gallery to see if they'd be interested in a collaboration. I'll be bringing these issues up. It would benefit you to be there, too."

Benny said nothing: only continued to drive the nib of his pen across paper, until it was a wonder it didn't rip straight through.

"Yes, Eliza," she mimicked through gritted teeth in the lowest voice she could muster. "Thank you ever so much for the help." And then, in her own: "Not a problem, Benny. Not a problem at all."

$$\infty\infty\infty$$

Benny knew that Eliza was right. He couldn't break even with his father once and for all if he didn't first invest in the money it would take to make the gallery successful. He was content in his little, unremarkable gallery — but content and unremarkable wouldn't get him what he wanted anymore. Still, the thought of entering Henry's office and seeing him in person this afternoon made him nauseous, and he could barely stutter a word when he got into Eliza's car later that morning to meet the artist Eliza wanted to collaborate with.

"Did you wake up on the wrong side of the bed this morning?" she asked as Benny slammed the door shut and thrust on his seatbelt.

It was no surprise that her car was probably about ten times more expensive than his own secondhand scrap of metal. It didn't whine in protest when she stuck the keys in the ignition, either, and there was no sickening whiff of petrol when it purred to life. It had been so long that he'd forgotten the subtle luxuries of wealth.

He ignored her remark, instead swallowed down his anxiety and glared out of the windshield. A light spit of rain pattered against the glass, the windscreen wipers swiping the droplets away in arched streaks. "Tell me about this artist we're going to meet."

"He owns a small, independent gallery down in St Ives focused on landscape prints. He gets a lot of tourists, so he sells a lot of paintings of the town, but he's looking to collaborate with more artists to vary his collection. He's particularly interested in your photography."

Unwilling to be convinced so easily, Benny hummed and

settled further into his seat. They rode the rest of the way swathed in a frosty silence, broken only when they meandered through the narrow streets of St Ives towards the car park. There were none near the gallery itself, so Eliza chose a spot atop a steep hill, overlooking the clustered buildings and roiling sea below. The breeze tasted saltier here, somehow, though St Agnes was just as close to the ocean. As they ambled down the steps and into town, Benny couldn't help but feel more than a little windswept. He tucked his hands away in his pockets, Eliza remaining beside him through cobbled roads and squawking gulls.

"Have you made your decision?" she questioned finally. "Will you be coming with me to meet with your father this afternoon?"

Benny raked a hand through his knotted, balmy hair, dodging a melting blob of ice cream in the middle of the street just in time. Despite it being early, the cafes were already packed with early risers devouring heaped English breakfasts and queuing for coffee. He dreaded to think how hectic it would be later on. "I suppose I don't have a choice."

"You have a choice," she said. "Make the right one."

There didn't feel to be a right one when it came to his father, but he said nothing, saving his breath for the gentle hike up to the shopping streets.

The gallery was a pastel yellow building opposite a fish and chips shop that already reeked of sizzling grease. A sign wafting in the light morning breeze titled it Coral Reef Art and Photography — and Benny ground his teeth against the reminder that he would need his own insignia soon enough. The fact that this gallery already had customers wandering about inside only proved it.

Eliza flashed him a pointed look. "Look at that," she whistled. "People. Perhaps you'll have those in *your* gallery one day."

"Not if you keep hanging around, scaring them away," he muttered in return.

Her heels clicked against the lacquered floorboards as they passed a row of framed landscape paintings and photographs to the front counter. They were... fine. Unextraordinary. Exactly what tourists with too much money on their hands would take home with them. Benny preferred more creative, abstract pieces that went deeper than the surface. But he supposed a few wouldn't look too bad in his own gallery. He couldn't imagine any of his photography here, though.

The person behind the counter was a neatly dressed, silver-haired man who looked just about ready to set sail on his yacht for the summer, with his pale linen trousers cuffed and blazer sleeves rolled to his elbows.

"Mr. Dean?" Eliza's spine straightened with an authority that Benny often found himself intimidated by. Though he could tease and joke well enough with their barbed, back and forth banter, it was becoming clear just how much Eliza had followed in her family's footsteps, and sometimes, she emanated all of the superiority Benny had run from long ago. "I'm Eliza Braybrooke. We spoke on the phone on Friday."

On Friday? Benny hadn't even agreed to her help then. Had she been so certain of herself that she'd planned all of this in advance? Irritation flooded through him, but he forced a tight grin when Mr. Dean introduced himself, offering a leathery, suntanned hand to shake. "Please, call me Scott. And you must be Benny."

Benny accepted it steadily. "I am."

"It's good to meet you. I've been dying to see some of your work in person."

At the mention of it, Benny pulled a plastic binder out and slipped it onto the counter. It contained his portfolio, thrown together in a rush last night.

"Benny is a very talented photographer," Eliza continued as Scott peeled the binder open and flicked through the pages. Benny could only shift uncomfortably on his feet, both from the unexpected praise and the fact that his best work was currently being scrutinised by another artist. "I think his landscape work would look beautiful in your gallery. It's a lovely place you've got."

"Thank you." Scott's nose wrinkled as he scoured the pictures. "Is all of your work edited monochromatically?"

"It's a style I like to keep to most of the time, yes."

He nodded, and Benny did not miss the way his mouth tugged down at the corners. When he lifted his attention finally, he peered at Benny over his rectangular, white-framed glasses perched on the bumpy bridge of his nose. Benny had to fight not to scowl.

"It's just a little depressing, is all. As you can see, my gallery is very colourful."

And very boring.

"Well," Eliza hesitated. "The different styles could actually compliment each other quite well. Benny and I were discussing the possibility of prints in the near future. Perhaps we could offer you some postcard-sized ones in exchange for the work you're willing to feature in Greystone Gallery."

Benny did not want this man's work anywhere near his gallery, but he nodded for the sake of politeness.

"I suppose it could work. Would you be willing to take commission for a new set of pieces incorporating colour?"

So that his pictures could merge into the plain background of the gallery? Benny almost scoffed at the idea.

"Mr. Dean, my client has a very specific style that helps to identify and distinguish his work. I'm sure you understand that."

It did not look as though he understood that at all. But Benny was more surprised that Eliza had jumped to his defence rather than agreeing to change everything he had spent the last few years refining.

"Quite frankly, Miss Braybrooke, I don't," Scott said. "And if I might offer my two shillings, neither will many others. Tourists do not come to galleries on the coast for artistic statements. They come for reminders of the beauty they see here, so that they can hang memories on their walls; to look back upon their days in the sun or to share it with their families. Your client will find it difficult to find an audience for his work in these parts if he's not willing to change it."

Benny opened his mouth to respond — but Eliza beat him to it.

"With all due respect, the best artists don't change their

style to fit other people's preferences. My client isn't here to cater to tourists. He's here because he creates things others don't have the talent or eye to. His work might not suit *your* tastes, but that's not a bad thing and it's unfair of you to suggest otherwise."

Scott absorbed the subtle scolding with a high-chinned, thin-lipped glare. It left Benny feeling awfully smug — though even more stunned now than he had been. He had thought Eliza to be the opposite of what she was; had expected her values to be similar to the arrogant arsehole's in front of them. But she understood Benny's style and wasn't asking him to change it.

An unexpected warmth blossomed in his chest at that fact.

"Very well," Scott said. "I suppose a few postcards would do no harm. These two will do." Scott's stubby fingers landed on the image he'd taken of the lighthouse along the headlands of St Agnes, and another of fragmented seashells on the beach of Port Isaac. Two of Benny's favourites. "Contact me when the prints are ready, and we can make a deal."

"Thank you, Mr. Dean." All of Eliza's sharp-edged hostility dissipated as she shook Scott's hand. "It was a pleasure to meet you."

"Likewise." Scott did not sound as though he meant it. In fact, Benny wouldn't have been surprised if the man wiped his hand on his fancy blazer after shaking Eliza's.

"Cheers," was all that Benny said, and even forcing that was a strain.

As they wandered back onto the damp, uneven streets of St Ives, Eliza muttered, "We won't be contacting him. Not a chance."

"Now who's the stubborn one?"

She rolled her eyes, arm brushing against his as she pulled a black umbrella from her bag and opened it to shelter them both from the drizzle. "You don't do pretentious artists. Neither do I."

Benny raised his eyebrows, and then schooled his features back to indifference. Even so, surprise continued to kindle in his stomach.

Perhaps Eliza Braybrooke was not quite as terrible as he'd thought after all.

Four

When he wasn't in London, Henry Weatherford worked in a looming block of newbuild offices opposite Torquay's spired town hall. The clock across the square chimed twelve as Eliza and Benny stepped into the building and passed the receptionist to get into the elevator.

Benny fidgeted beside her as they made their ascent, and she began to wonder if anxiety was contagious when her own belly began to jitter. She had no idea what she had gotten herself into, wedged in the middle of with Henry and Benny — only that Benny had shut down with the mere mention of him yesterday and hadn't spoken of his father since. The morning had been spent trying to avoid his glum gaze despite the faint kernel of concern in the pit of her stomach. Concern and guilt. It felt as though she was doing something terrible in bringing him here today.

It was the dinner last night that caused it. She had sat down with both Henry and her own father, Gerard, completely oblivious to the fact that they'd formed some sort of partnership. And then they had told her over their plates of peppered duck that Gerard wanted to get a share of Greystone Gallery; that they would be taking it over together. She wasn't sure where that left Benny, and didn't have time to wonder now.

When they reached the top floor of offices, Eliza gave her name to the assistant there, and the two of them waited on a set of chairs to be called. Henry's office sat in the corner, the door closed — for now.

Benny continued to jitter beside her, jiggling his knee up and down as he chewed on his nails.

"Benny," she said softly — and had no idea how to follow it up but with: "It's going to be fine." She wasn't sure she believed her own words.

Benny only scoffed, scraping his messy hair off his face and smoothing down his beard.

And then the assistant called them in.

They entered to find Henry perched on his grand, mahogany desk, wearing a pleasant grin that faltered only slightly at the sight of Benny. "You didn't tell me I would have the pleasure of my son's company today."

When it was clear that Benny was not going to respond, Eliza said, "Well, we have some things we'd like to talk about today that require your input. I thought it would be helpful if we were all at least in the same room to discuss the gallery."

Henry raised a bushy, greying eyebrow but nodded nonetheless, adjusting his tie as he offered the seats opposite before sinking into his own. Eliza took one. Benny hesitated behind her before he did the same.

"Are you going to say anything, son, or are you going to keep shooting daggers at me like a brooding adolescent?"

"Father," Benny ground out through gritted teeth. The tension between the two men turned taut, a rope pulled tight enough that she could feel each fibre splitting and fraying. A tug of war, with Eliza somehow thrust right into the middle of it. "Good to see you."

"I doubt it." Plucking a pen from his blazer, Henry glared back at his son. "A phone call and a visit in the space of a week. I think it's the most I've heard from you in years."

Eliza had never seen a parent look at his child that way. Her own mother and father were difficult at times and didn't always approve of her choices — particularly the ones that kept her well within the plus-sized clothing sections in Ralph Lauren — but they had never held such poison, such shame, in their eyes at the mere sight of her.

What had Benny done to cause it?

"Well, you insisted on involving yourself in my business," Benny retorted.

"The business I fund, you mean?"

Eliza cleared her throat, placing her purse by her feet. "Anyway, I thought you'd like to know, Mr. Weatherford, that Benny and I are working together to curate a more... organised and appealing exhibit than the one that currently stands. We've discussed the first steps, and we're in the process of scouting new artists to collaborate with."

As though remembering Eliza's presence, Henry relaxed in his chair and smoothed his composure, though his thumb still ticked wildly around the pen's cap. "Very good. I trust your judgement."

"The problem is that the gallery appears very understated from the outside, too." Eliza glanced at Benny, giving him his open to take the reins. He didn't. He was too busy staring at something on the desk.

A photograph propped beside Henry's nameplate. Eliza recognised two of the three people beaming from it: Henry, clutching a baby-faced Declan in his arms. The other was Benny and Declan's mother, a brunette woman she had never had the time to meet. She had passed a few years before Eliza had met the Weatherfords — probably not long after the picture had been taken.

She scanned the office and found no other photographs of Benny. As though he was not a part of the family. As though he didn't deserve a spot at Henry's desk with the rest of his loved ones.

"Elaborate, please," Henry ordered.

Eliza had forgotten she'd even been talking. Heat prickled her cheeks as she continued shakily. "Well, there's no sign outside, so passers-by probably wouldn't even know it was a gallery in the first place. It also has poor lighting inside, which means the art won't be viewed well."

"That's no good, is it, Benjamin?" Henry clucked his tongue, goading.

Benny's gaze flicked up to meet his father's, and Eliza nearly balked at the hatred seeping into those warm, brown eyes.

"I work with what I have," Benny said.

"Which doesn't sound to be a lot. What do you plan on

doing about it?"

Eliza cut in, "Obviously, w —"

Henry lifted a hand to shush her. "Apologies, Miss Bray-brooke. I'd like to hear from my son on this one."

Cheeks spattered red, Benny sucked in a breath. Eliza's own heart leapt to her throat. She had never felt such thick, oily tension before, not even between Benny and Declan. This was different. The way that Henry glared at his son, and the way that Benny glared back... They were two edges of the same sword, both sharp enough to cut clean through glass.

"Clearly, some improvements need to be made." Benny's voice was a brittle rasp.

"And how do you intend to make them?" It sounded more like a challenge than a question, and one that Henry surely already knew the answer to.

"Eliza has explained to me that to make a profit, some money will have to be invested into the gallery first. Money that I don't have." He shuffled uncomfortably, picking at a piece of skin around his thumbnail.

Henry hummed as though he understood perfectly — and delighted in it. The corner of his mouth quirked up into a smarmy smirk.

"Since the gallery is your investment," Benny continued, "I wondered if you might be willing to invest a little more for the sake of the improvements. That way, business has a chance of getting off the ground and I can pay you back as soon as possible."

"I might have known you'd only show your face where money is involved. Some things never change, do they?"

Benny's nostrils flared. Eliza fought back a cringe, crossing her legs to shrink herself slightly. She wished she could speak up for the sake of the gallery, for the sake of breaking that steely tension, but she wouldn't risk being reprimanded by Mr. Weatherford again.

"I suppose not," Benny replied.

"Send over the invoices for the new assets. We can add them to your very long list of debts, can't we?"

"I'll pay them back." Determination glittered across his features, jaw quivering before it set.

"I've heard that before. I suppose I won't be getting a thank you, either." Henry cocked his head, waiting.

Benny practically choked out his gratitude, focus straying to Eliza for only a moment. She had a feeling that if she hadn't been there, things might have gone quite differently. "Thank you."

The satisfied grin snaking along Henry's lips left nausea churning in Eliza's stomach. She'd signed up to help make the gallery more profitable, not help a father grind his son beneath his thumb. This wasn't right.

"Are we done here?" Benny had turned wan beneath his dark beard. He rose from his seat before Henry had even the time to utter out his reply.

"Anyone would think you didn't want my help."

Having the good sense to stay quiet, Benny only marched out of the office, leaving the door to swing on its hinges behind him before giving its final slam. Eliza winced, half-expecting the frame to splinter against its wrath.

And then it was just the two of them, marinating in an uncomfortable silence. She swallowed down her unease, scrutinising the elder man with her hands clasped in her lap. She'd always thought him a little intimidating... but had never taken him as *this*. Cold-hearted. Evil. Her mother had always had the utmost respect for Henry, and Eliza had had no reason to contradict that. Indeed, as soon Benny left, Henry's callous expression smoothed — but those eyes remained cold beyond the surface, still. Ice posing as water.

"You haven't told him," she found the courage to say. "He doesn't know, does he?"

"Know what?" It was a challenge; one that Eliza had no intention of cowering away from. She felt tricked, somehow, to have been put in this position. Stuck between her father and Henry on one side, and Benny on the other. It hadn't been her place to divulge anything more than her own part in it — and even if that wasn't true, she wouldn't have wanted to. She was already too entangled in this, and still digesting what *'this'* was.

"He doesn't know that you plan on handing the gallery over to my father."

If Henry felt any guilt, he did not show it. "I will not be handing the gallery over to anyone. Your father and I came to a mutual agreement. He has far better capabilities of managing the place than my son."

"I'm not comfortable with lying to my client."

"Benjamin is not your client," he reminded coolly. "I am. You're most welcome to tell him, but I doubt he will be quite so... *cooperative* if he knows the gallery won't be his for much longer. It would be in your best interests to keep your nose out of that which does not concern you, Miss Braybrooke."

Eliza's heart wrenched — with guilt, with sympathy, with fear. She had only found out about her father's plans to become partners with Henry and manage the gallery last night, long after Benny had agreed to her help. It had been sitting on her like a barbed weight ever since. She had already seen what the gallery meant to him. He had no idea that his father planned to take that away. It didn't feel right. She had already told Gerard, her father, as much, but he wouldn't hear any protests.

"You should tell him the truth."

"With all due respect, I know my son better than you. He would sooner burn the place down than be pushed out of it. I will tell him when the time is right. Your only job is to prepare the gallery so that the transition runs smoothly."

Eliza hesitated. She didn't want to look Benny in the eye everyday and lie. She didn't know if she even had it in her to do so.

"Do I have to call your father and tell him that a new curator is needed?" Henry asked — *threatened*.

Her stomach roiled. Her father had paid for her education. He had taught her, raised her, to be the woman she was now. The *curator* she was now. If she couldn't even curate the gallery he was set to manage... She wasn't sure she could deal with the disappointment that would follow. Once her father got his heart set on something, he would get it through hell or high water regardless of who he had to trample over in the process. He was like Henry in that respect, though usually far more subtle about it. It had been made clear at dinner last night that neither of them held any concern for Benny's place in all of this. The gallery was all that mattered. The gallery, and the money.

If Eliza backed out now, she doubted Henry would stay quiet about it. The reputation she had spent the last eight years building would be tarnished. Half of her clients knew the Weatherfords. The other half knew her father. She would lose work if she didn't revamp the gallery into a profitable business. No one in her professional circle would care about the reasons behind it; would only see the ways she had failed. She would lose everything. Her entire career was based on good reviews and connections.

"That won't be necessary." She hated herself for that mousy, pathetic act of submission, and for the fact that she was not the type of woman who could just walk away when something wasn't right. But she had no idea who Benny was or why his father wanted to do this to him. It was none of her business.

Her only business was what Henry and her father wanted from her. She would not risk everything for the sake of a man she barely knew.

She would do what she had to do.

Five

Benny was already halfway down the road when he realised that he had nowhere to go. Eliza had driven them here. Unless he wanted to pay for three trains back to St Agnes with money he didn't have, he was stuck. He continued walking toward the seafront, anyway, claustrophobia clinging to his skin like a slimy film as he weaved through afternoon shoppers. Above the busker crooning a U2 song on the corner, he almost didn't hear his name being called.

Almost.

He turned, shoulders slumped and hands fisted in his pockets. Eliza's bright figure springing towards him was easy enough to spot: a splotch of metallic gold against the drab grey. She stumbled against the uneven stone as she caught up to him, breathless and rosy-cheeked and clinging onto his arm to steady herself. "Where are you going? My car's parked back up the road."

"I needed a walk," he muttered flatly. His blood still simmered with an anger he had never been able to snuff out; an anger that always seemed to fester and infect until it was all he had, all he was. It had been worse today. His father had snatched away a world that Benny had tried to keep for himself. The gallery was the only thing that had ever truly been his, and now Henry had tainted it.

Worse still was the fact that Eliza had been there to witness every moment of it. He couldn't look at her now because of it, even when she almost coughed up a lung trying to regain her breath.

"Look... I'm sorry," she rasped finally. "I had no idea it would be like that."

"It's not your problem." Benny shrugged, sounding calmer than he felt. "Don't worry about it."

Eliza frowned and worried at her bottom lip, pale eyes piercing into him until he squirmed against their intensity. "Are you hungry?"

His stomach had been grumbling for the last hour, but he didn't say so.

"*I'm* hungry," she continued. "Fish and chips?"

"Shouldn't we get back?"

Eliza drew the sleeve of her blazer up to check her wristwatch. "We have time. There's nothing else we have to do today."

The last thing that Benny wanted was to hang around his childhood hometown any longer, kilometres away from his father's office. But he *was* starving and Eliza was giving him puppy dog eyes...

"Okay. But you're paying."

"So chivalrous," was all that Eliza mumbled.

They found one of the lesser seagull-soiled benches on the seafront — as far away from the marina and Benny's memories as possible. Still, he couldn't ignore the white smattering of houses curling across the coast's tail, towering above the town. It was the street he had grown up on, his house the highest of them all. Millionaire's Row, others called it. Millionaire or not, he'd hated every moment of living up there.

Eliza *had* paid for the salt and vinegar-drenched chips, though Benny had argued with her in the middle of the shop for a good five minutes about it. He didn't know why. Clearly, she had a hell of a lot more money than him.

He wondered if she still lived on the opposite side of the bay, in that grand house they'd ran around in as kids, or if she had moved on, too. He couldn't bring himself to ask. He couldn't bring himself to say much of anything, too busy still stewing over the meeting with his father as he chewed on his lunch.

"What happened?" Eliza asked finally, spearing two chips

with her plastic fork and popping them both into her mouth. He'd been surprised at her choice of meal; had expected her to turn her nose up at anything that was served in sheets of newspaper instead of a shiny, white plate. "With you and your father, I mean. Why don't you get on anymore?"

"We never did." Benny avoided her gaze, eyes remaining on the choppy ocean ahead. The sun was attempting to bleed through the clearing clouds, the breeze warm on his face though the world remained damp from the earlier showers of rain. "Hasn't my brother told you everything, anyway?"

"Declan doesn't talk about you often."

"I suppose he wouldn't." Talk of his brother curbed his appetite, and he slid the chips away in favour of his coffee.

"Meaning?"

"Nothing," he brushed off, scratching his scalp and sinking lower. They sat on opposite ends of the bench, coffees and newspaper wrappings and all of Eliza's silent questions between them. "I'm sure all of your hoity-toity friends have plenty to say about what happened with me and my family, anyway."

"I've heard rumours," she shrugged. "Stupid things. Nothing believable."

He smirked bitterly, not surprised in the slightest. "They're probably true."

Eliza's eyes narrowed as she chowed down her last chip before slapping her hands free of the salt. "You ran away to start a rock band and had an affair with a groupie?"

"Alright, maybe not," he snorted. "I'm not that interesting — or desirable."

She grinned at that, eyes the same blue-grey as the incoming tide. It only occurred to him then that she had been probing him; had wanted to make him laugh. He faltered as he met her gaze, something fluttering against his ribcage that he didn't want to acknowledge.

"So?" she said. "What happened? Why did I stop seeing you around, rock bands and love affairs aside?"

Sweat began to gather on his palms. If she knew, she

wouldn't want anything to do with him. He sipped his coffee to slow down his response. "You're full of questions today."

"I just endured a very tense game of piggy in the middle with you and your father. Forgive me for being curious."

At the reminder, shame flooded him and set his cheeks blazing. What must she have thought of him after that? He'd felt like a submissive mongrel bowing to his master in that office, so desperate for his father to just agree without making it difficult. Without making him feel like a pathetic beggar. He was sick of needing his help. Sick of being so useless and lost and inferior. "A lot of people have tense relationships with their family."

"That wasn't just tense," Eliza observed. "It was brutal."

"Well, my father is a brutal man."

"And I suppose you've never done a thing wrong."

Benny clenched his jaw, focus falling to a splash of blue paint on his frayed jeans. "I've done plenty."

She went quiet, then, but he could still feel her gaze burning into his neck. "The way he spoke to you... I wasn't expecting it."

He hadn't, either. He never did. He'd spent years and years of his life thinking that next time would be different. That one day, his father would start treating him like a son, even if Benny wouldn't give him any reason to.

The day hadn't come.

"It's just the way it is with us," he said.

A ridge puckered between Eliza's brows. "But why?"

Benny could only shake his head and grapple for an answer that would satisfy her enough to drop it. "Because it is. Because I'm the family embarrassment. Why does it matter so much to you?"

"It doesn't," she stuttered. "I was just curious. I don't understand."

"You wouldn't." Venom laced his words, and he hated himself for it — and yet couldn't clamp down what he said next. "You're probably exactly what your parents hoped you would be. Perfect, rich, successful, snooty."

"Why am I snooty, Benny?" Eliza snapped. "Because I have a

real job? Because I brush my hair more than once a week? Because I don't throw tantrums? God, grow up."

A fresh bout of anger prickled beneath his skin. He threw his coffee cup in the bin beside him and then balled the newspapers into tight balls and did the same with them. "You always have to stick your nose in where it doesn't belong."

"You know," she scoffed, "I liked you when we were kids. You were moody and quiet, but you were still kind. Now you're just an arsehole."

"I could say the same of you," he replied through gritted teeth.

The crashing waves were suddenly too loud, the white houses above too blinding against the midday sun. He couldn't stay here. He couldn't remember all of the reasons why he had hated this place. It felt as though just being here had already caused that loneliness, that rage, to crawl beneath his skin again, turning him back into a man he hated.

"Can we go, please?"

"We'd better, before I push you into the sea myself," she retorted, standing without another word and marching back across the seafront.

Benny threw her rubbish away before the wind did it for him and sucked in an exasperated breath before following her, the clicking of her heels the only sound either of them made until they got back to the car.

Six

Eliza had barely spoken to Benny since their argument yesterday. Any guilt she had felt about lying to him had dissipated — or, at least, was easier to push away now. Her first impressions of him had been right: he was a self-entitled arsehole who prided himself on being difficult. It was easier to get the job done without him finding out and making it harder for her. Why Henry hadn't already fired Benny and saved everyone the hassle, lies, and deceit that would only come later, she couldn't fathom.

They'd spent the morning in another artist's studio space a few towns over. This one had been a young woman named Fiona who Benny had liked enough to agree to a collaboration. It was at least a step in the right direction. Eliza spent the rest of the afternoon in his gallery, the two of them aggressively sighing from their separate corners of the room every so often to remind one another that they were still annoyed and still not talking.

That palpable tension only popped when Benny began dragging something out from the storage room at the back. Eliza hadn't been in there yet, but Benny had told her yesterday that if she needed any extra frames, she could help herself.

He was not bringing out extra frames now, though. He was bringing out chairs — and easels. And canvases.

She put her pride aside for long enough to ask, "What are you doing?"

"Setting up," he grunted beneath the weight of the stacked chairs.

"For?"

"Classes."

Eliza puffed out an irritated breath, hands digging into her hips. "Can you please elaborate on your monosyllabic answers?"

"Oh, sorry." He shot her a sharp glare before arranging pots of paints and brushes, setting some down at each easel. "I suppose I can't keep up on the days. I didn't know we were back to talking."

"If you're back to being a jerk, don't bother."

"I didn't realise I'd ever stopped." The corner of his mouth curled with a sardonic smirk. Eliza would have liked to slap it off. "I run classes on Tuesday evenings for anyone who wants to turn up."

This took her aback. Benny had never mentioned classes before. She'd been certain that he spent the entirety of his days standing behind that desk, drinking coffee and sketching to pass the long, customerless hours. She still had yet to see what it was he drew, though his fingertips were always blackened by charcoal. "You teach?"

"It's not really teaching."

Eliza cocked her head curiously. "Then what is it?"

"It's…" Benny tugged at the curling ends of his dark hair as though nervous, and then slotted the last canvas onto its easel. "It's therapy."

"Therapy," she repeated. The word held no weight. She didn't understand.

Humming, Benny disappeared back into the storage room again. This time, he emerged with his laptop — an old grey slab of peeling stickers and broken hinges. The CD drive flopped in and out as he carried it over to the desk.

"Explain."

He straightened and looked at her for the first time since yesterday. Something in her stomach swooped and jolted, though she had no idea why. "I don't believe that you haven't heard of art therapy."

"Of course I have."

"Well…" Benny lifted his eyebrows as though he'd said something glaringly obvious. "That's what I do. Not many people can afford therapy, or they find it difficult to talk to a stranger, so I hold sessions for people who are struggling or recovering and need a place to… well, to vent. To let it out. Kind of like a support group, I guess."

Eliza frowned. "Don't you need a qualification for that?"

"I have one."

None of it made sense to Eliza. If he was holding classes every week — and successful ones, she gathered from the dozen easels he'd set out — how was the gallery still struggling to stay afloat? "How much are the classes?"

"Zilch."

She almost choked with disbelief. "You do understand that this gallery is making absolutely no money, yes?"

"Yes. Thank you for reminding me."

"So why aren't you charging money?"

"Unbelievable," Benny breathed under his breath.

Eliza's features twisted in disdain. "What?"

"Nothing. Just that everything's about money for you, isn't it?"

"Oh, don't get on your high horse again," she bit back. "You're running a business with absolutely no profit. What do you expect me to say?"

"Funnily enough, this is *exactly* what I'd expect you to say."

Though the words were not said any more viciously than his other remarks, the statement sliced through Eliza like a hail of bullets. He always made her out to be so cold, so heartless, so haughty, as though he was any better. As though he knew anything about her at all. It was no wonder that his father was going to hand over the gallery to Gerard. Benny clearly couldn't run a business for the life of him. She opened her mouth to say as much, but the venom died on her tongue when the gallery's door swung open with only the second visitor today.

But it wasn't a visitor who stood in the threshold, a perfect, toothy grin splashed across his face. It was Declan.

Eliza had thought that Benny had been tense before. She realised now he had not even been close. His whole body seemed to seize up in the presence of his brother, his dark features rolling with the first black clouds of an oncoming storm.

Declan inspected the place with little interest as he stepped in, still clad in his work suit. "This is… cosy."

"Declan." Eliza forced a pleased smile, though unease rippled through her. "What are you doing here?"

"I'm picking you up for our date."

Eliza flinched, digging the heel of her palm into her forehead. Declan had asked her out to dinner after the exhibit on Saturday, and she had agreed without much commitment, assuming that he was just engaging in his usual harmless flirting. She hadn't so much as thought of him since. "I completely forgot. I'm sorry."

The younger Weatherford sauntered over to Eliza like a peacock puffing out its feathers, slinging his arm across her shoulder just as he had at the exhibit. Just as he seemed to every time he was in Benny's presence. Was he trying to *claim* her? Why? Benny had no reason to care about their non-existent relationship. "Has my brother been keeping you busy? There's certainly a lot of work to do here."

"It's coming along. Slow and steady." Eliza watched Benny carefully as she spoke. He did not even look up from where he glared at his laptop. "I need to finish up here. Why don't you wait for me in the car?"

"And miss out on all this beautiful art?" Declan motioned to the wall nearest, where nothing hung but metal hooks and lights. Eliza had taken the pieces down earlier today to decide which ones were worth focusing more attention on.

She shot him a warning look. "I'm parked up the road. I'll be out in five."

The sloppy, overbearing kiss forced onto her temple was the last thing that Eliza had been expecting, and she would have cringed away from it had he not still been gripping her arm. She was glad when he left, waving at her a final time through the window.

"I suppose I'll see you tomorrow."

Benny gave the slightest nod. "Yep."

So they were back to not talking, then. Eliza rolled her eyes and scooped up her purse, pretending that her stomach hadn't tangled into a tight knot after their conversation. "Great."

∞ ∞ ∞

Eliza didn't have the heart to tell Declan that she didn't like sea-food. He'd taken her to a flashy place on the pier, lit by rustic bulbs hanging above them and kept warm by outdoor heaters. The last remaining strip of light glowed across the sea behind him, blind-ing enough that she could get out of looking at him too much. Not that he was bad to look at. It just felt... awkward.

"This is new." She sipped her wine and tossed the prawns around the plate to find the pasta hiding beneath.

"I think it's been open for a few years now, actually," Declan responded through a mouthful of lettuce. With the salad dangling from his lips, he looked an awful lot like Pickles, the overweight rabbit she'd gotten for her seventh birthday, and she had to stifle a laugh behind her wine glass.

"I mean this. You. Picking me up and taking me to dinner."

"It's been a long time coming," Declan shrugged and pulled out his phone. He'd done the same thing every five minutes since he'd stepped out of the car, barely looking up for long enough to notice Eliza's steely disapproval. She had liked Declan once, and had liked the constant game of flirting they'd been playing since they were teenagers, but Declan was... Well, he was bland. Boring. They didn't like the same things and never had anything to talk about. And in all the years they'd been doing this, he'd never asked her out properly like this. She couldn't help but wonder if Benny had something to do with it. Sibling rivalry, perhaps, since she was spending more time with the older Weatherford. Perhaps Declan was threatened — by what, she couldn't guess.

She only hummed her unconvinced agreement, tucking her billowing hair away from her face as the breeze almost up-rooted the faux roses placed in a vase between them.

"So..." It was an effort to find something to talk about, espe-cially when all curiosity led back to Benny. She couldn't help but ask about him. "What happened between you and your brother?

The two of you used to be so close."

Declan let out an ungraceful snort through his nose, sawing at his battered cod. "He's a prick. I'm sure you've noticed that, too."

"Did something happen to drive you all apart?"

"A long time ago. He accused Dad of all this crazy shit out of nowhere."

"Like what?" Eliza stopped eating to lean closer.

"About how he cheated on Mum before she died. He was a bloody drunk, always picking fights for no reason. Then we heard nothing from him until he..." Declan trailed off and tugged on his earlobe as though he'd said something he shouldn't have.

"Until what?" She didn't know why it mattered; why she was prying. And yet she couldn't stop. Benny was a puzzle she couldn't quite piece together. The way he reacted, the way he seemed to shake with anger when he saw his father and stiffen with his brother... none of it was normal. If she was going to get thrust in the middle of it all, she at least wanted to understand why. Who, exactly, would she be dealing with when the truth came out?

"He's always getting Dad to sort out his problems when it's convenient for him." Declan's voice wavered, eyes darting anywhere but at Eliza as crimson crept from his collar, up his neck. "And then he'll go back to hating us when he's gotten what he wants. He's a complete and utter mess. Dad should just cut him out and be done with the waste of space."

Ice slithered through Eliza. No matter what her family did, no matter how they annoyed her, she could never imagine talking about them that way... *Hating* them that way. Declan spoke of his brother as though he was a piece of old, chewed up gum clinging to the soles of his Burberry loafers. Benny might have been difficult, but did he deserve that? Was he *that* bad? She couldn't imagine it.

"Excuse me." Declan wafted his hand to flag down a waiter, still chewing on the food in his mouth. A skittish teenager scuttled over immediately. "There's a bone in my fish."

The bone, pinched between his thumb and forefinger, was no thicker than a strand of hair. The waiter blanched, and sympathy began to well in Eliza. "I'm sorry, sir. There's always a risk of a few bones with fish. It does specify that on the menu."

"I could have choked on it." Declan shoved the plate away dramatically. "I'd like to request a refund."

"*Dec*," Eliza scolded, but if he heard her, he didn't acknowledge it.

"Since you've eaten most of it, I don't think that will be possible, sir. Can I offer you a free drink?"

"You mean this cheap wine?" The white wine swished as he raised his glass. "This service is shocking. We waited for over five minutes to be seated. Fifteen for the food to come out, and it was lukewarm at best. If you won't reimburse me, where can I make a complaint?"

"Er." The young boy's knuckles whitened against the menu clutched in his hand. "I'll go and get my boss, sir. Just a second."

"Good. While you're there, tell the chef that the fish is dry. He'd better keep an eye out for any jobs going at McDonalds."

The boy looked as though he might burst into tears, his face turning beetroot red. Eliza could only sit back and cringe until he'd left, ashamed to have witnessed such a thing without a word. But she'd been too shocked. Too disgusted.

"Was that necessary?"

They had an audience, now. Diners around them cast disbelieving looks their way, followed by sour tuts of disapproval.

"I'm paying a small mortgage for this bloody meal. It would help if they hired competent staff."

Eliza's own cheeks flamed. Any hint of respect she'd had for Declan vanished. She might have enjoyed spending her money, but she would never demean somebody else in the process. The poor boy would probably be hiding somewhere, traumatised, now. "You're being rude."

Declan only dug back into the fish he had just made a complaint about. It only confirmed the fact that Eliza would not be suffering through a second date with Benny Weatherford's brother — ever.

Seven

"How was the date?"

It took Benny about six hours to work up the gall to ask, though he wasn't sure he really wanted to know what Eliza and his brother had gotten up to the night before. Things hadn't been quite so tense with Eliza today, though they still had the occasional tiff about where she had put a painting or why he'd been feeding his breakfast bagel to a stray cat at the door.

"Fine," was all Eliza replied with — and then frowned when she turned from her laptop, where she had been tending to some emails, to find him dragging in a few pink, heart-shaped balloons. "Is it the wrong time to tell you that Valentine's Day was months ago?"

"They're for singles night."

"I'm afraid to ask," she deadpanned.

Benny put a balloon in each window before he responded. "It's a St Agnes thing. Every so often, the community centre and local pubs hold a night for all of the sad little lonely hearts around town to socialise. The rule is that if you're single, you put a balloon up in your window."

"You have two. Is that a sign of being doubly, desperately single?"

"One's for you," he jested, tugging on the balloon's string to watch the heart bob around before he returned to the desk. Surprisingly, she didn't move from where she leaned on the other side, still concentrating on the laptop screen with her plump bottom lip between her teeth.

Her beauty struck him at random, sometimes — an inconvenience if ever there was one. She didn't even have to try, and yet... she was all golden and soft features, blonde hair spilling like sunlight across her face. He had to remind himself often that she was a snob who probably hated his guts, beauty be damned.

"What makes you think I'm single?"

"You're dating my brother. The only loving relationship he's ever had is the one he has with his bank account. You're either painfully single or losing your mind."

"We're not dating." She glared, fingers tapping against the keyboard idly for a few moments as though she was debating something. "Benny?"

"Hmm?" Benny had been shading in one of his doodles in his notebooks — a buttercup he had sketched yesterday without thought. It only occurred to him now why the flower had popped into his head.

Her.

He paused now, glancing up to find her staring absently at him.

"Never mind."

"Spit it out."

"Have you ever ordered food and it doesn't come out as you wanted it to? Like, for instance, you find a bone in your food or the... I don't know, the potatoes are dry."

He suppressed a chuckle at the sheer randomness of her. "Hasn't everyone?"

"Do you usually complain to the waiter?"

"Is this some sort of metaphor for Declan's shortcomings?"

"No," she tutted. "I'm just asking if you've ever sent back food or made a complaint at a restaurant."

"Not unless it's raw or growing fungi." He raised an eyebrow, starting to grasp what it was she was truly asking. "I take it Dec wasn't happy with his meal last night."

"How—?"

"I know my brother too well. He's been pulling that stunt to impress women since his first date. Thinks it makes him an alpha male. Probably learnt it from my father."

Eliza wrinkled her nose. "He almost made the poor waiter cry. I didn't know what to do."

"You mean you weren't charmed by an adult man throwing a tantrum in a public place?" He gasped dramatically. "Shocking."

She smirked, resting her chin in her hand and shutting the laptop closed.

"What's the deal with you two, anyway?" It was an effort to sound nonchalant as he went back to sketching — on a fresh page with no buttercups. Talking about Declan made him feel sick, and yet it was all he'd thought of last night. Benny couldn't forget the image of his hands around Eliza's waist; couldn't help but wonder how close they were getting while he sat in his shoebox apartment alone. "Haven't you been flirting since high school?"

"I suppose. My mum would love it if I brought him home. I think our parents want us together more than we do."

"But?"

Eliza sighed. "But it's always… weird. And let's face it, I'm probably not his type, and I don't think he's mine."

Relieved, Benny grabbed a stack of leaflets from his drawer before slipping one over to Eliza. Advertisements for singles night. He hadn't bothered to keep them out, since nobody had visited the gallery today, anyway — again. "It's your lucky day, then."

She inspected the leaflet, features twitching with amusement. "Are you going?"

"Why? Are you asking me out?" He smirked, though something in him tightened. Perhaps a small part of him wanted her to say yes — to coming, that was. Not to asking him out. Of course he wouldn't want that.

Eliza rolled her eyes. "No. I need to know if I'll have to avoid you."

He only shrugged. "I'm helping out at the community centre. I'll keep an eye out for the man of your dreams, shall I?"

Eliza shook her head wryly, and Benny tried to ignore the hope rising in him — an uninvited guest in the soft centre of his chest.

He couldn't.

∞∞∞

Apparently the majority of singles in St Agnes were old-age pensioners — but that didn't stop a few of them from flirting with Eliza, men and women alike. She wasn't entirely sure why she had stayed in the first place, other than the fact that she had nobody to go home to save for her aloof, sleepy cat, Kahlo. And perhaps she was a little bit curious to see if Benny was so rude to everybody in town, or whether he saved it for Eliza only.

As she sipped her orange juice, watching him sway along to the wistful notes of 'Moonlight Serenade' with a tottering, bubbly old woman who's sunken cheeks glowed rosily from all the attention, Eliza began to suspect it was the latter. Still, their laughter warmed her heart, even as she reminded herself that he was not as kind as he appeared now. Even if a part of her wished she could dance with somebody that way; have fun that way.

"Has Dorothy stolen your fella?" A broad, northern-accented voice beside Eliza startled her enough to drop the roasted peanuts she had been scoffing from the small bowl on the table. A red-haired, grinning woman she had noticed at the bar earlier had sidled into her booth. "She's a minx, that one."

Eliza's lopsided grin was both amused and confused as she swept the nuts from her lap. "Benny is definitely not my man. Dorothy is quite welcome to him."

"Oh, sorry. I thought with the way you were looking at him that maybe singles night had at least been a success for someone." The woman popped a pretzel into her mouth, casting Eliza a pointed look as though she was not a stranger but a friend who knew her too well. Eliza couldn't stop the heat from creeping across her cheeks, as though she had been caught doing something she shouldn't have.

Had she been staring? "Didn't I see you come in together?"

"Yes, but we're just..." *Friends*, she had been about to say — but that was a lie. "I'm helping him curate his gallery."

"Ah," the stranger nodded in understanding, "I keep meaning to pop in there. Still, he's sweet, isn't he? I think Dorothy's a bit in love."

Eliza returned her attention to the makeshift dance floor. Benny still danced with the grey-haired woman, twirling her under his arm slowly while she sang along to the music. It *was* sweet. But was it real? She felt as though she'd met a million different versions of him, and she had no way of understanding which he truly was. "You know him, then?"

"Everyone knows everyone in this town," she replied. "I'm Sadie, by the way."

"Eliza."

They exchanged a smile, and Eliza thought that she quite liked Sadie — the accent, the colours, the constant smile on her lips. "Uh, oh. Lydia has just discovered the only eligible bachelor in the room."

Indeed, a leggy, dark-haired woman marched over to Benny confidently. He stopped dancing as she whispered something in his ear. Whatever it was must have been good because he waved Dorothy away before being dragged to the table, where mostly juice had been laid out in plastic cups.

A twinge of something sharp stabbed through Eliza's chest, and she hated herself for it. Why should she care who Benny talked to?

"Are they seeing each other?" she asked with as much nonchalance as she could muster.

Sadie snorted. "Lydia wishes. No, Benny hasn't dated for a while, now. I think his last relationship hurt him more than he let on. I suppose that's not really my business, though."

Even if that was the case, he seemed happy enough laughing along with Lydia as she brushed an invisible fleck of lint off his shoulder. Eliza shifted, turning so that her back was to them and she'd no longer be tempted to watch. "Do you fancy getting a real drink?"

Sadie's eyes brightened, and she nodded eagerly. "Please. Let's go somewhere with less pensioners and more beer, please."

The proposal sounded perfect to Eliza.

∞∞∞

Benny had not seen Eliza all night. One moment, she'd been chatting to Sadie in a booth in the corner. The next, they'd both disappeared. He knew he shouldn't care, but his attention kept straying from Lydia's talk of single-parenting and her son's problems at school. He couldn't stop looking for Eliza, wondering if she'd gone home or simply ventured out to one of the other pubs in town.

He couldn't blame her. He and Lydia were the only people below the age of fifty in the community centre, and the pensioners were beginning to file out as the night wore on. Benny's own feet ached from all of the dancing, though he hadn't minded entertaining the women. He took the first opportunity he could to wish Lydia a goodnight and shuck on his jacket, stepping out into the damp night before he was cornered again. The pub across the road still teemed with laughter and music. Any other time, he would have avoided it at all costs, but when he rounded the corner, he found Eliza's car still parked up. It didn't feel right to go home without at least saying goodbye.

His pulse sped up when he was swallowed by the noise and lights of the bar. He hadn't been anywhere near one in years, now, never quite trusting himself. His muscles grew taut, knees locked, as he weaved through familiar faces, the musky stench of sour ale burning his nostrils and churning his stomach. Old memories, old versions of himself, resurfaced in a barrage of images and feelings — hatred. For the drink, for himself.

But it dulled slightly when he found Eliza perched on a stool by the bar, her back to him. Sadie still sat beside her, downing a frothing pint as Niall, the town's favourite bartender, laughed at something one of them had said. A spike of something else, something hot and irritating, spread through Benny at the sight; a diluted version of what he'd felt when Declan had picked her up from the gallery yesterday.

He rounded the bar, brows raising when he found Eliza with a mostly empty glass of wine in front of her. "Having fun?" he questioned, leaning casually, as though his heart was not thundering in his chest.

"Benny!" Sadie sang, eyes already unfocused. Thankfully, Eliza seemed only slightly merrier than her usual self — proven by the fact that she smiled at him. Not falsely or sarcastically, either, but sincerely. Her cheeks puffed with it, eyes glittering, and he wanted to see it again, wanted to see it always. She had never looked at him that way before.

"Do you want a drink?"

"No, no." He lifted his hands quickly. "I just came to say goodnight. How are you getting home?"

"Oh, bloody hell!" Eliza slapped her forehead dramatically, almost spilling the last dregs of her drink in the process. "I forgot about that. I'll have to get a cab."

"That will cost a fortune," he countered.

"Benny is a chivalrous man." Sadie's mouth curled with cunning, though she could barely spit out a word with so many syllables in her current state and the word sounded more like 'chilavous'. "He'll drive you home. Won't you, Benny?"

Benny narrowed his eyes at the woman before checking his watch. If he drove Eliza home, now, he would be out until way past midnight, and he was already exhausted from an early morning of scouting a new artist. Besides, the last thing he wanted to do was force Eliza into his grotty, pathetic little car. The rusty engine would probably conk out before they even made it out of St Agnes.

"*Or*," Sadie continued just as Eliza opened her mouth, no doubt to protest, "why don't you just stay at his tonight? It will save you another trip here tomorrow, won't it?"

If he was too embarrassed to have Eliza in his car, he was certainly too embarrassed to have her in that tiny apartment above the gallery.

"I could try to find a hotel," Eliza suggested.

"It's summer," he said. "You won't find a vacancy at this time of night."

"Well..." Eliza hesitated, gnawing at her lip. "An Uber should be fine."

Only it was dark outside, and Benny had heard horror stories about women catching cabs late at night. He couldn't, in good conscience, let Eliza get into a car with a stranger, not knowing if she'd get home safely. He only had two options — and only one of those two made any logical sense.

He sighed, scratching at his beard uncomfortably and trying to ignore Sadie's glittering eyes on him. It wouldn't surprise him if the woman was trying to play matchmaker — though why, he had no idea. He'd only dated a friend of hers not that long ago. "It would make more sense to stay at mine. Your car's here and you'll be back tomorrow, anyway. I'll crash on the couch for the night."

Eliza's brows drew together. "I really don't mind catching a cab."

"Well, I do," Benny grumbled. "It's a long drive. It's not all that safe. I'd rather you stay."

She pondered this, fighting against Sadie's hands already urging her off the stool.

"Go on," Sadie crooned. "Everyone loves a good sleepover."

Benny was surprised when Eliza nodded in defeat, slipping off her stool and straightening out her skirt. They said nothing as he led her out, though sweat was already beginning to bead along his hairline — and it wasn't the alcohol that caused it this time.

It was certainly the strangest St Agnes singles night he had ever experienced.

Eight

"Sorry the place is a mess. I wasn't expecting company."

After seeing the way Benny had flirted with Lydia in the community centre, Eliza found that hard to believe. The apartment was a bit of a mess, though, with clothes strewn over the sofa and dishes unwashed by the sink. An easel stood by the window, canvas only half-blank. She couldn't make out what the whites and blues were supposed to be yet. She wanted to know; imagined how he must stand here, paint-stained and taut with concentration, or perhaps loose as he let the paintbrush speak for him.

There was so much of him she didn't know yet, but she felt just a little bit closer to finding out standing inside his home.

"Why don't you ever put your paintings downstairs?" She had only ever seen Benny's photography in the gallery, but up here, there were a dozen small oil paintings piled and hung wherever there was space. They weren't grey and shadowy like his photographs. They were full of colour and life — emerald seas and fields of buttercups. Autumn trees and snowy mountains. "These are... They're beautiful."

Benny had been whizzing around the living room, tidying up his things, but he stopped behind her now. For once, there was no teasing in his tone when he said, "Thank you."

"So why hide them?" she pried again, turning to him. A bundle of T-shirts spilled from his arms.

"I'm not hiding them. I just... It's difficult to explain. You wouldn't understand."

Eliza scowled at that, crossing her arms over her chest. "Right. I only did a degree in art history."

"Well, that's exactly it," he huffed, placing the clothes down on the kitchen counter in defeat. "I took plenty of photography courses. I know what I'm doing with that. I know what works and what doesn't. But painting is different. I paint because I enjoy it, because it helps me. I don't do it to be good at it or to sell it."

Perhaps she could understand that. It had been a long time since she had pursued something for the pleasure of it. Painting used to be the same for her, until her father had made it clear that she wouldn't be successful — or wealthy — as an artist, and she would be better off with a different role in the industry.

For the first time in a long time, her fingers twitched with the need to curl around a brush and just... paint.

"Fair enough. Still, I think these are worth trying to sell."

"Maybe," was all that Benny mumbled before chucking the clothes in the washing machine.

"Sorry about tonight," she said, if only for something to break the silence threatening to encroach. "I don't know what I was thinking."

"It's no problem." He flicked the kettle on, resting against the kitchen counter with a crooked smirk. "I must admit, I didn't think you were the type for spontaneous bar trips and unplanned sleepovers."

"This isn't a sleepover," she retorted, rolling her eyes. "I haven't had a sleepover since the age of nine. Besides, I *am* known to have spontaneous fun every now and again. And Sadie was nice. I had fun."

Benny's hum was barely audible over the boiling kettle.

Resting her elbows against the breakfast bar, Eliza dared to glance up at him through thick lashes. "I hope I didn't ruin *your* sleepover with someone else."

"And who would that be?" Benny frowned, though Eliza had the feeling he already knew and just wanted her to admit that she'd noticed.

And she would. She was in no mood for games tonight, too curious, too unsure as she tread this foreign, unexpected territory with him. She was in his *apartment*. In his town. Had stayed tonight because he'd invited her. None of it made sense to her.

"That pretty woman swooning over you in the community centre."

"Dorothy?" His eyes glittered with the taunt. "She's a bit old for me, I think."

Eliza's answering look dripped with sour amusement. "The other one. You know who I mean."

"Why? Are you jealous?" The kettle whistled to a boil, steam curling across Benny's face as he poured the water into two mugs.

"You wish," she scoffed, even when her stomach answered with a searing spark of confirmation.

He sobered in an instant, draining her tea bag quietly. Eliza scowled when he used the same spoon to stir his coffee before throwing it in the sink. "I'm not interested in pursuing anyone at the minute."

"Or is no one interested in pursuing you?" She regretted her words immediately.

Benny's eyes darkened, mouth pulling down at the edges as he slid her mug over to her. "Is it that obvious?"

"I…" she stuttered, guilt clawing through her.

"It's fine." Benny's hands curled around the mug, though it wasn't the least bit cold in here. In fact, Eliza was starting to sweat. "You're right. Dating is… difficult. I'm sure you know that, what with seeing my brother and all."

She didn't want to talk about Declan anymore. "But Lydia seemed willing enough. Did you at least get her number?"

"No." He sipped his coffee, though it must have been scalding still.

"Why not?"

"I told you. I'm taking a break from all that."

It made no sense. He claimed that nobody was interested, and yet when they were, he wasn't interested. Eliza furrowed her brows, though she didn't quite know why it mattered to her so much. Sadie's words came back to her. *I think his last relationship hurt him more than he let on.* She hadn't believed it then, but she saw that sadness swimming in his eyes now and wondered if she'd been wrong about Benny being the callous, pretentious brother.

She only knew that she had never seen nearly as much emotion in Declan. She had never been able to read those eyes and know what they held as she could now with Benny, despite the brothers being so similar. But where Declan threw his money around and bullied waiting staff, Benny danced with old ladies and involved himself in the community.

None of it made any sense at all.

"Why?" was all she could ask — again.

"You don't want to know my relationship problems."

Yes, she did. Too much. "Well, you know enough about mine. It's only fair."

Benny sighed, raking a hand through his thick hair. "I just don't think I'm made for a relationship, alright? I'm just the guy who everyone wants to be 'casual' with," he air quoted. "I can't seem to find anything deeper than that."

"Because you don't want to?"

"Because *they* don't want to."

Eliza pressed off the counter and slid onto the stool instead, skepticism colouring her features. "Maybe you just haven't found them yet. There were plenty of women at the bar tonight. Perhaps you should have fended off your beloved elders and joined us."

The tightening of his jaw was so subtle that she shouldn't have noticed it. But Eliza couldn't stop noticing. She couldn't stop trying to read him, to understand him. Who was he? Not the man his family thought he was. Not the man *she'd* thought he was. Not tonight, anyway. "I don't do pubs."

"You don't do relationships. You don't do pubs. You don't do money. What *do* you do, Benny?"

Benny chuckled, slurping a final glug of his coffee before sitting the striped mug down on the counter between them. "Wouldn't you like to know?"

She did. She really, really did.

∞ ∞ ∞

Eliza could smell Benny on his bedsheets and his shirt, and it made her hot and restless and... confused. She couldn't stop thinking about him. Her heart still hadn't stopped racketing against her chest; her reaction made worse because he was having a shower with only two doors between them.

He'd told her to help herself to his clothes if she needed something to sleep in. With her curves, she had expected nothing to fit her, but the first paint-stained flannel she came across brushed almost to her knees, and she'd had to roll her sleeves up or else look like a child wearing a lumberjack's clothes. It was the first time she hadn't felt too big in a long time. Usually, she was so aware of just how much space she took up, and though she had long since stopped wanting to shrink herself, it still felt nice.

It was an effort not to press the collar to her nose every few seconds, just to smell that spice and musk again as she made herself comfortable in his bed, feeling... not herself. She did not sleep, bare-legged, in other men's beds. She did not wear their shirts or accidentally drink too much that she couldn't get home.

She only felt more separated from herself when the door creaked open and Benny poked his head in. "Sorry. I forgot my pyjamas. Can I...?"

"Of course."

Warmth stirred between her thighs when he wandered in with only a towel hanging from his waist. He wasn't what she expected — his body was softer, like hers, but still broad and sturdy. Rivulets of water trickling from the damp ends of his hair and down through the crests and valleys of his torso. A tattoo of an arrow lanced across his ribs, chest hair damp and dark, and Eliza could not breathe as her eyes sank to the lines half-hidden beneath the cushioned pouch of his belly. He turned his back to her to root through the dresser, and she forced her gaze away with burning cheeks.

"Did you find something for yourself?"

"Just a shirt." He turned with plaid lounge pants in his hand, eyes shifting from her face to the shirt she wore — and darkened. He knew what she had implied; that she wore nothing else.

Her chest panged with the knowledge that he seemed to be just as interested in her half-nakedness as she his. "Thank you."

"No worries." His tongue slid out, swiping across his bottom lip as he shook his hair of stray droplets. "Goodnight, then. Sleep well."

"Benny?"

He had been leaving, but he retreated now, waiting expectantly.

"When's your next art class?"

He only let his confusion show for a moment. "Next Tuesday. Why?"

"I'd like to go. Just to see what it is you do."

Surprise flickered in his eyes, throat bobbing beneath the stubble. "Yeah?"

Eliza nodded and meant it. Benny was a mystery to her, still, and if her heart was going to leap in her chest every time he walked into the room, she would at least do everything she could to figure him out.

And hopefully figure herself out in the process.

Nine

The gallery's sign had been drilled onto the wall on Friday — gleaming silver letters reading 'Greystone Gallery' centred across the uneven brick above the door — and already, tourists had begun to flock in. Benny had even sold a couple of paintings by some of the local artists, and though he'd been feigning professional indifference afterwards, Eliza hadn't missed the secret, proud grins he'd been trying to hide every time she turned around.

His reaction made her feel terrible. Benny still had no idea that his father planned to hand the gallery over to Gerard; that it wouldn't be his for any longer. It felt slimy and wrong to keep it a secret, and yet it was too late to quit. She wished she had in Henry's office that day, but then what? Benny would still have his gallery snatched from him, whether she was involved or not.

But if she told him, at least he'd be braced for the betrayal.

She tried to wipe her mind of it when Benny began to set the chairs and easels up the following Tuesday afternoon and she took to helping him. He seemed… jittery. As though having her sit in on the lesson was making him nervous. She supposed she'd earnt that, with all of the judgement she'd passed over him the last few weeks.

"So you said this was like a support group."

Benny's brows furrowed as he straightened a canvas on its easel, tongue poking out in concentration. "Kind of, yeah."

"A support group for what?"

Abandoning the wonky canvas, Benny straightened to look at her. "Well, anything. Family problems, mental health issues, addictions. For some people, this is the only place they have."

"What made you set it up?" That curiosity still gnawed at her. It never seemed to stop.

Benny released a sigh — not of annoyance, she didn't think, but as though he was preparing himself for something. Those brown eyes glittered. Haunted, she had thought once, and she saw that same darkness in them now. It made her want to reach out — to do what, she didn't know.

"We all have our problems," is all that he said.

Any other questions she'd been meaning to ask would have to wait. Three men bumbled into the gallery, and a dazzling smile split across Benny's face.

"Look at you with the snazzy sign outside! Has it always been there?" the short man in the middle asked, patting Benny on the shoulder lovingly. He didn't *seem* troubled — but then, not many people wore their hardships all over their face. She knew that well enough. If Eliza was being honest with herself, she had been expecting women to walk through the door rather than three stocky, rugged looking men. Most of the men she knew would never feel comfortable admitting their struggles, let alone joining a support group — and one in an art gallery, no less.

"No, Jim," Benny chuckled. "We're having a bit of a revamp. *Apparently*, the gallery needs a few changes." He eyed Eliza pointedly, and she smirked. "This is Eliza. She's my new curator, but she thinks she's my boss."

"I am his boss." She cast a small wave at the three men, all of whom ogled her without much shame.

"I'm Jim. This lanky thing is Andy." Jim gestured to the tall one on his right, fair-haired and beak-nosed. "And this one's Grant. He talks absolute shite, so don't talk to him." The man on his left was darker, like Benny, though clean-shaven and more muscular.

"Oi!" Grant protested, shoving Jim playfully.

"Take no notice of any of them," Benny dismissed, though a smile still played on his lips. "They're all as bad as each other."

"I bet none of them are as bad as you," she teased.

Another group came in before Benny could argue, this one four women. Two of them — Cheryl and Mel, they introduced themselves as — were older and immediately set to laughing and joking with the men, the other two slightly more timid. Eliza greeted them quietly, finding those same shadows she had recognised in Benny. The final three to show were two more women and a middle-aged man. Eliza watched intently when the man pulled Benny aside to talk in private. From where she stood, she couldn't hear the low mumbles being exchanged, so she took to pouring apple juice and water for the new arrivals. Benny had set up a plate of biscuits, too, and as people began to sit down at their chairs, he played a soft instrumental playlist from his battered laptop.

Eliza took the seat furthest from the front, while Benny remained behind an easel, the gallery his stage and the new visitors his audience. She had never seen so many people piled into the place at once. It felt... right. Alive.

"Alright, let's get started." Benny clapped his hands together and then wrung them anxiously. "Thank you all for coming again this week. As you've probably noticed, a few changes are being made to the gallery, but these lessons aren't going anywhere."

Another wave of guilt scraped through Eliza's stomach, until the juice she'd drank earlier tasted bitter on her tongue and she wasn't sure if she could keep it down for much longer.

"Anyway, it's good to see you all. Is there anything anyone wants to get off their chest this week? Nothing's off-limits. This is a place where we paint what we want and say what we want, remember."

Benny picked a paintbrush up and mixed it in his own palette, and the others followed — including Eliza. She had been desperate to paint for a while now, and didn't feel that stifling pressure to be good at it in these four walls. She watched the others, first: in front of her, Jim splattered random bursts of red and yellows on his canvas, and a black-haired woman who had introduced herself as Aisha smeared blue across hers.

Nobody said anything as the tinkling piano instrumental drifted around the gallery.

"Okay," Benny said, still focused on the painting in front of him. "I'll start. I..." He cleared his throat, eyes shifting above the canvas, to Eliza. It lasted only a moment, but still she was certain her heart had come to a standstill. "Well, I went into a pub for the first time since I stopped drinking. It was hard and the temptation was there, but... I was okay."

"Proud of you, mate," Andy praised at the front.

And Eliza... Eliza had stopped breathing as Benny's words rearranged themselves a dozen times over in her head. *Sober. Pub. Temptation.* He'd been an alcoholic. While she had been studying art history at Cambridge and chasing her dreams, Benny had been... what? Passed out at a bar? She had heard the rumours that Benny had gone 'off the rails,' as her mother had put it — that he'd left home to spend his days crawling around pubs — but that was just one of many. She hadn't believed it, just as she hadn't believed any of them. Maybe that was just because, with her silly little crush, she had always taken him to be quiet, thoughtful, kind. After all, Benny was a Weatherford, and why would a Weatherford have any reason to stray from the pristine family image, what with all the wealth and success they inherited?

But maybe Eliza had been wrong about all of it. Maybe *this* rumour might have been true.

The thought made her heart wrench, made worse still because *she* had been the reason he'd gone into that pub last week. If something would have happened, it would have been her fault.

She couldn't paint, couldn't move. She could only sit with her brush suspended in midair while everyone else continued as though his words held no weight. Even Benny did not look up again as he thanked Andy. And then Grant began talking of his own struggles — gambling and debt and that constant need to fall back into old habits.

From there, everybody joined in — mothers who had lost their children, anxieties and disorders, chronic illnesses and problems that Eliza had never even thought about before. Her own troubles felt pathetic in comparison, so she sat back and said nothing, feeling like a privileged idiot unworthy of sharing a room with such strong people.

But Benny knew exactly what to say. He knew when to nod and when to offer advice, when to agree and when to use his own experiences as comfort. And Eliza knew that everything she'd thought she'd known about him had been wrong. Kindness seeped through his every action and word, his every smile and every blink. He offered the gallery as their safe haven, told them that it would be open for them always, anytime. After that, a new silence descended — one that was not weighty or smothering, but liberating and fresh as winter air. Brush strokes danced in time with the mellow music, and they laughed at any mistakes or spilled paint. Eliza remained an outsider, and was happy to be. These people needed each other. She would not intrude.

Nobody showed their work at the end — not to Eliza, anyway. Jim was proud enough to shake his canvas in front of Benny's face before he took it home, cradling it in his arms. Aisha displayed hers, too, and Benny asked if he could hang it in the gallery. Pride swelled on the woman's features, eyes glittering with tears as she nodded. The others wished them a goodbye and left with their paintings — everybody save for the man who had pulled Benny aside earlier. Eliza had learned during the session that his name was Glen.

She had noticed that Glen appeared more weathered than the rest of them, and hadn't spoken much unless asked a question. Again, she couldn't hear what he said to Benny, and to avoid seeming nosy, she began to drag the chairs back into storage.

When she emerged, Glen was gone.

Benny remained silent as he packed up with her, refusing to meet her gaze. All of the awful things she had thought of him, said to him, felt like a poison she wished she could rid herself of, and she had no idea how to put that into words.

"Is Glen okay?" she questioned finally, quietly, gathering the last of the paintbrushes and slipping them into a pot.

Glassy-eyed, Benny broke out of the daze he'd been lost in and paused the music on his laptop. "He's struggling at the minute."

Eliza nodded, unsure of what to say. "I'm sorry, Benny. I had no idea —"

"It's not your fault," he interjected quickly. "The pub, I mean. You couldn't have known."

Because he hadn't told her. Why would he? She'd done nothing but judge him since the moment she'd stepped through the door. "What you do here… It's wonderful. Really."

Benny shrugged modestly and piled the collapsed easels away. He stopped when he came to hers. Her painting still sat there. "Do you mind if I peek?"

Pulse thundering, Eliza tensed. It had been a long time since anybody had last seen her work — a long time since she had even painted at all. And a long time since she had last felt so insecure. "Only if I'm allowed to see yours."

"Deal." Benny rounded the easel — and paused. She wandered to his side, trying not to scrutinise every flaw and smudge and distortion in her work. It was the outside of Greystone Gallery that she had painted, all red-bricked and charmingly crooked as it baked in the St Agnes sun. The new sign hung above the door, and a silhouette lingered in the window, her attempt at depicting Benny. Because it wasn't Greystone without him.

She knew that, now. And she wouldn't let Henry or her father take it from him, not if she could help it. She would tell them of these lessons, of the good he was doing, and they would listen.

Eliza would make it her mission.

Benny's lips curved with an astonished grin, brown eyes glittering. "You drew the gallery."

"It's not very good, but…"

"Is that me?" He pointed to the broad frame in the window, words bubbling with an amusement contagious enough that Eliza had to suppress her own laughter.

"It is."

"Eliza…" The way he whispered her name almost brought her to tears. She wanted to hear it again and again, wanted him to say it until it lost all meaning. "This is amazing. Really, it is."

She flushed despite herself, inching ever so slightly closer until their arms brushed. "I don't know about that."

"I want to hang it up in here. Could I?"

"But it's rushed and messy." She frowned.

"Who taught you that art was supposed to be anything but rushed and messy?" he asked. "Cambridge?"

Cambridge and her father. It hadn't occurred to her that somebody might find beauty in her wobbly lines and accidental splatters. She didn't know why. It wasn't as though every painting, every artist, she had studied had been perfect. Perfect didn't exist in the art world — and yet she had expected it, had been taught to expect it, of herself. Why?

"You really like it?"

"I love it," he admitted. "Really. It'll look brilliant in the window."

"Okay," she breathed. "Then yes. Of course. If that's what you want."

Benny beamed, and gone was those shadows, those sagging shoulders weighed down by things Eliza couldn't imagine. She wanted that joy burned into her memory for all of the giddiness it brought her. She practically skipped over to Benny's painting, no real inkling of what she would find there.

A loose sprinkling of buttercups merged into one another on his canvas, smattered in yellows and greens. They reminded Eliza of summer and childhood; of holding the wildflower to her friends' necks to see if they liked butter; of freshly cut grass and scorching sunshine; lemonade and the coconutty scent of sunscreen. "I'll trade you. My painting for yours."

"You want it?"

She did. She wanted to wake up to it every morning. She wanted the time to analyse every stroke, wanted the memory of this conversation, of Benny. "Well, I already know you're too stubborn to sell it. What do you plan on doing with it?"

"Most of the paintings I do here end up in storage," he admitted.

Eliza had known that already, though. She had noticed at least thirty canvases gathering dust and cobwebs in the back room earlier.

"This is too good for storage. I want it."

"You want it?" he repeated, incredulous.

Eliza gave an aggressive shake of her head. "Yes, I do. It's only fair."

"What are you going to do with it?" Benny raised a skeptical eyebrow.

"Burn it," she mocked with a roll of her eyes. Benny did not laugh. "I'm going to hang it up."

"You, Eliza Braybrooke, are going to hang *my* painting up in your house?"

Eliza planted her hands on her hips. "Yes! Is it so hard to believe?"

"Isn't that space reserved for all of those fancy schmancy artists you like?" He took the canvas off the easel and placed it on the floor to fold away the stand. "I think my one-hour attempt at a basic flower might pale next to Monet."

"Please," she scoffed. "I don't have *Monet* hanging in my apartment. This is good, Benny. It deserves to be appreciated."

His brows furrowed, and he squinted at Eliza, closing in on her until she could smell the coffee on his breath. "Did you hit your head on one of the storage shelves earlier?"

Eliza tutted, but made no move to back away. She could feel his warmth, and it only clawed through her when his fingers sifted through the roots of her hair as though checking for the non-existent injury. She froze, and then he did, too, tingles prickling around her scalp and then tip-toeing down her face, her jaw, her neck.

If he touched her, kissed her, now, she would let him.

But he didn't. He staggered back, hand falling to his side at an awkward angle before raking through his own hair. Eliza only realised then that her lips had parted. She pressed them together quickly, sucking in a jagged breath and hoping Benny had not noticed how intensely she had *wanted*.

"I should get going. I, er... I'll see you tomorrow." She grappled for her purse and the still-wet painting. "Thanks for letting me sit in."

"No worries," Benny muttered absently, a muscle quivering in his jaw as he watched her run around the gallery to collect everything. "Drive safe."

Eliza wasn't sure she would be able to — because when she left the gallery and hopped into her car, she still thought only of him; of how close he'd been to her and how different he'd seemed and how... *good.*

She thought of him for a long time after, too.

Ten

Eliza did not drive into St Agnes alone the following Monday. After asking Henry to schedule another meeting with her — and her alone — the older man had offered her a ride there to see for himself how the gallery was all coming along. A sleek black car had picked her up from her apartment, and she'd spent the following two hours beside the hard-faced businessman while they crawled their way through morning traffic.

"Mr. Weatherford," she said now, not before clearing her throat of its crackling nerves, "I've been meaning to discuss something with you. Now feels the perfect opportunity."

"Well, we have nothing better to do in this godforsaken traffic," he bit out tersely. "Bernard. Might we hurry up a bit? I'd like to get there before dinner time."

"Stuck in the morning rush, sir," Bernard, the driver called from the front in a thick, cockney accent.

Henry sighed his disapproval and crossed his arms. "You were saying, Miss Braybrooke?"

"I know that my father has his heart set on Greystone, sir, but I've come to realise that Benny really is trying his best with it."

His lips curled in unpleasant surprise. "That may be, Miss Braybrooke, but his best and my best are very different things."

"You don't understand," she blurted — and immediately regretted talking to him so freely. But she couldn't stop. She couldn't spend another day lying to Benny. "Benny is doing a lot of good for the community, and business has been much better since the sign went up. I really, truly believe that Benny is the best man for the gallery."

"Haven't I already entertained this conversation once? I thought we agreed then on what was best."

"But I didn't know then," she countered desperately. "You see, Benny uses his gallery to run art therapy classes every Tuesday evening. It's really quite remarkable —"

Henry's raised hand silenced her. "Is your father aware that your loyalties have changed, Miss Braybrooke?"

Eliza wrinkled her forehead, frustration rolling through her in hot waves. "My loyalties haven't changed, Mr. Weatherford," she said, steely as she dared. "My insight has. You hired me to offer my professional opinion in order to make the gallery successful and profitable, and I'm giving it. Your son is talented. He has potential. But he can't do that without his gallery. He deserves a chance. I have every intention of telling my father the same thing."

"You may discuss what you like with your father, but it won't change a thing. I have made my decision."

"May I be frank, Mr. Weatherford?"

Henry's only show of affirmation was the subtle incline of his head and the clench of his jaw — not that Eliza had needed it. She would have continued with or without his consent. Her heart was in this now. She couldn't let Benny lose the gallery, couldn't let that group of people she'd met last week lose their support, their joy, their source of peace. For some, it was all they had.

"You are doing this for money. For profit. You've made that clear. My father knows his art, but he doesn't know St Agnes. He can bring a million new artists in, and it won't do a thing for your funds. People, tourists, in that town... they don't want another gallery of high art they'll never be able to afford. They want somebody they know. Somebody friendly and modest. Somebody like *them*. Benny only wants to use his work to help people. He doesn't care about prices or profit. He understands the purpose of art better than anyone I've ever met. Don't take that away from the people who need it. Please."

She was breathless when she finished — and yet Henry seemed not to have heard her at all. His cold eyes were on the growing queue of traffic behind them again.

She had never known a man like him before. Somebody

who did not want his child to succeed. It made her feel ill to be in the same enclosed space with him, the smell of his expensive cologne catching the back of her throat.

She might have been dismissed for now, but Eliza would try again. She would say it a million times over until it stuck.

The gallery was Benny's. She would make sure it stayed that way.

∞∞∞

The gallery had been Benny's sanctuary; a place where none of his old wounds could touch him. That sanctuary crumbled to ash when his father walked through the door, chin tilted obnoxiously in the air.

No.

Benny's chest tightened at the sight of Henry, looking haughty and unimpressed and incongruous against the colourful art. He shouldn't be here. He *couldn't* be here. He didn't belong. This wasn't his. It was Benny's. And yet Benny felt as though it was all slipping through his fingers, and he could only gawp — until Eliza followed in behind his father, sheepish and apologetic.

Henry did not bother to greet his son. Instead, he wandered straight over to the blank wall — the only one that had not been filled yet. Everything else had been covered with new and old art alike. The photography by the front. The portraits on the right wall. Landscapes on the left. Oil paintings and pastels and ink. And Eliza's painting of Greystone sat in the centre of it all, on a new divider that would soon showcase the artists of St Agnes. Henry chose not to see any of it.

"There certainly needs a lot more work to be done."

"We plan to visit a few more artists this week, Mr. Weatherford," Eliza responded, following at his heels like an overbearing puppy. "We already have three collaborations set up with other independent galleries around Cornwall, and we have plans to donate some of our landscapes for an exhibit —"

"Is this what we're calling art these days?" Henry interrupted — and Benny's heart sank. His father had wandered back to the front, to Benny's photography, to scrutinise what he no doubt knew to be his. "A three-year-old could have done this."

If he was stronger, braver, Benny would have found some way of replying. He would have defended himself. But he had never felt strong or brave beside his father, especially not when it came to his work — work he knew Henry would never understand. His father was not an artist. He was not even an art lover. All he saw in this gallery was the money he'd invested and the profit he hoped for, with the added benefit of another opportunity to tear down his son.

Henry shifted to the landscapes, lips pressed into a grim, uneven line. "It's no wonder business is slow."

"Business isn't slow, Mr. Weatherford," Eliza argued. "As I mentioned in the car, Benny has had three new buyers this week alone, and the gallery has had more visitors than ever. Once we finish all of the exhibits and offer prints and postcards —"

"None of it will be enough. This gallery does not even have the space it needs to be successful. It's nothing more than a ramshackle little cottage, just like every other building in this irrelevant town."

"A gallery doesn't have to be big to be successful," Benny finally mustered the courage to chime in, his gruff voice echoing off the walls with more force than he'd expected of himself. "My goal was never to reach the masses. This place is for local, struggling artists who need somewhere to showcase their work."

Henry turned on his heel to face Benny, cocking his head with a fierce glower. "And how exactly will that pay your debts, Benjamin?"

"You never cared about my debts before." Benny's fingers flexed at his sides, but he kept his voice firm, even, as he rounded the desk so that he was in full view. "You never cared about the gallery at all, and you don't know the first thing about art. You were just happy to throw your money at me and hope it would keep me well away from your perfect little family. What's changed?"

Henry's eyes turned to stone. "One gets tired of leeches eventually. Don't you think it's time you stopped living off my generosity?"

Benny snorted at that. *Generosity*. As though Henry had a generous bone in his body. "Isn't that why you sent in the cavalry? The gallery is improving. People are coming. I'm doing everything you asked of me. Is it not enough?"

He knew the answer to that already. Nothing would ever be enough. Not for Henry.

"Eliza tells me you have been using my space as a free-for-all for your vagrant friends. Is that true?"

From his periphery, Benny noticed Eliza suck in a breath, face paling. Betrayal thickened his blood to hot, sticky tar.

He had introduced her to his friends and their struggles. He had let himself be vulnerable, had shown her who he truly was, and had thought she'd been accepting of it. Had thought —

Face burning, Benny swallowed down the bile in his throat and forced himself to meet his father's eye for the first time. No more fear. No more shame. He wouldn't cower anymore. "I run classes for a few friends once or twice a week. What's it to you?"

"At what profit?"

"None."

"It's embarrassing, Benjamin." Henry clucked his tongue, scouring the paintings again. Aisha's hung there now, a myriad of warm colours that suited her personality perfectly. It didn't deserve to be torn apart by Henry's steely eyes. Henry did not deserve to be in the same room as it. "Airing your troubles for the town to see and encouraging others to do the same. What sort of man does it make you?"

He could only hope the answer was a better man than his father, though it had not always been the truth. "Our values are different. It doesn't make mine wrong."

"And yet only one of us runs a successful business."

If being cold and detached and selfish made him successful, Benny did not want it. He would rather be back on the streets than turn out anything like his father.

"Mr. Weatherford," Eliza began, "if you could just see —"

"I think I've seen enough." Henry cut her off, glancing at his wristwatch absently. "I expect a substantial increase in profit in the next two weeks. Should you deign to show up to my annual soiree, we shall discuss our next actions from there."

Benny had not been to one of his father's snotty garden parties since he'd left home, and certainly had no plans to now. They'd been the bane of his existence growing up, suffering through classical music and bland canapes and adults whose favourite hobby was to talk badly about others, until he'd taken to hiding in the linen closet all night. "I won't be attending."

"It would be in your best interests if you did." It sounded like a threat; one that only made Benny's jaw clench tighter,until his face ached. "There is some business I wish to discuss with you there."

"And I suppose your office won't do?"

"On this occasion, no. Until next time, Benjamin." Henry nodded first at Benny, and then Eliza. "Miss Braybrooke. I'll have my driver pick you up at four, shall I?"

Eliza only gave a weak nod in response.

Benny waited for the relief when Henry finally left, but it didn't come. His chest remained tight, crushed, his stomach still twisted into a million different knots. The gallery was no longer his, and he hated it. He hated all of it.

He hated his father for taking all of that security, that peace, away again, after he had worked so hard to get it.

"I'm going to head down to the beach. I need some fresh air," he mumbled, throwing his camera around his neck before Eliza could argue.

"Benny." Eliza's voice was a mere whisper, and one that could not pull him out of the shadows.

"I'll be back later."

He left her there, hoping that the sea air could cleanse what the gallery no longer could. It was the only way of escape he had left.

∞∞∞

Eliza waited fifty-seven minutes before she gave in and set out to find Benny — and it was fifty-seven minutes longer than she'd wanted to wait. After closing the gallery, she wandered the narrow streets of St Agnes, following the directions of crooked arrows on leaning signposts until the nearest beach came into view. A wretched, guilty ache had long since settled in her stomach, the memory of Benny's features twisting with betrayal as Henry had torn him down replaying in her mind over and over. She could only imagine how broken he'd be if he knew the truth.

Eliza would do everything she could from ever letting that happen.

The sun was hidden behind stagnant clouds, the promise of rain dangling in the air. It at least meant that the beach wasn't too busy. Eliza slipped off her heels before ambling into the sand, the grains chafing between her toes. It had been a long time since she had walked barefoot across the beach. She was always too busy working these days.

It made her feel like a child again, hair taken hostage by the briny breeze while the sea sang to her. A Border collie barked at the crashing tide, chasing a ball into the ocean. Another family built sandcastles by a cove, and a couple of surfers rode the waves in the distance.

And there, face hidden behind the lens of his camera, Benny stood beneath a stone arch, water pooling around his ankles and his jeans rolled halfway up his calves. Eliza's stomach churned again, but she swallowed down her fear, raking her hair back from her face as she met him.

The sea was ice cold as Eliza slipped her feet into it, toes catching slimy seaweed and sharp pebbles. Benny didn't seem to mind. He didn't seem to want to look at her, either, though he at least let his camera fall to his chest to tuck his hands into his pockets. The lines of his face were more pronounced in the wash of daylight as he stared out to the grey horizon.

She hesitated, watching as water puddled in her footprints. She opened her mouth to ask if he was okay, but then thought better of it. Of course he wasn't. She wouldn't have been either if her father had talked about her art that way. Gerard at least had the courtesy of letting Eliza down gently.

"I'm sorry," she settled on finally. It felt as though she'd been apologising a lot recently.

"For what?"

"I thought that if your father saw the good you did, if he knew... He would change his opinion of you."

"My father isn't the sort to change his opinion," Benny muttered.

His flannel shirt wavered in the wind like a plaid-patterned flag. The same shirt Eliza had slept in not that long ago. The blue paint stain still spattered the breast pocket. Had he not washed it since then, or was it just an old mark stuck there for good? The thought left her hot, flustered, and she remembered how it had felt to fall asleep that night wrapped in the smell of him. How she had enjoyed it. How he had walked into his bedroom in nothing but a towel, and it had left her feeling wrung out and strange and wanting.

"Benny," she whispered, and she didn't know why. What could she say? What could she do? She'd made a mess; a mess she was still caught in, still trying to fight her way out of. What was she *doing*?

"He decided I was a waste of space a long time ago." Benny's dark eyes finally flickered to her, glistening with a sadness that left Eliza feeling like a cracked, hollow vase of dead flowers. She wanted to wash it away. Wanted to reach out and find a way to make it better. "I appreciate you trying to help, but that won't change."

That was it? He wasn't angry at her? Eliza frowned; shifted. No longer able to hold back, she drew her hand into his, fingers lacing and palms brushing. His were not calloused or rough like the rest of him, but smooth as silk despite the paint and charcoal sullying them. Artist's hands. "He's wrong. We'll show him that. There's a first time for everything."

Surprise parted Benny's lips, and she hated that her compliment elicited such a response. As though he did not expect someone — *her* — to believe anything good about him.

"But he isn't, Eliza. I'm…" He freed his hand to scratch the crown of his head uncomfortably. She felt his absence immediately; felt stupid for even reaching out to him in the first place. "I'm no good at this. You know that."

"No," she replied. "I don't know that."

"You said as much yourself."

"I don't care what I said before we knew one another. I've seen the good you can do. I've seen the art you can make, the art you want to show to the world. It deserves to be appreciated."

She rooted through the bag slung on her shoulder then, pulling out a stiff envelope she'd been itching to show him all morning. She handed it to him, and he took it warily. A stack of prints and postcards fell out when he emptied it, his nimble fingers catching them just before they could fall to the sand. All of them were black and white and beautiful. All of them were his.

"I wanted to tell you earlier. I had some prints made for you to sell."

"You did this?" Benny scanned through them with nothing short of awe.

"Yes. Because they're good, Benny. People will buy them."

Finally, he lifted his gaze — and Eliza almost stopped breathing altogether. Everything he felt, everything that would never be able to be put into words, danced across his face — the opposite of the hatred and sadness she had seen in that gallery.

She realised then what she had already somehow known all along: that Benny was not the terrible, entitled failure his family loved to label him. He was just a man who cared about art. A man who had been stuck under his father's thumb for too long, crushed and shrunken and deserving of far more.

"I don't care what your father thinks," she said, and meant it. "I know that this gallery — *your* gallery — will be successful. I know it because you're talented and passionate and kind, and I'm going to help you."

Rising to her tiptoes, Eliza hooked her hands around his neck. He bowed his head, and she was so close to kissing him. But his lips didn't find hers. It was his forehead that brushed against her, eyes fluttering closed — pained. Relieved. She couldn't decipher which emotion it was, and suspected it was a bit of both.

But she would keep to her word. She would rid him of that pain. It was a vow she made to herself and to him, silently, but she was sure he felt it when his breath hitched and their chests touched. His arms snaked around her waist, and then she was engulfed by him, her head propped on his strong shoulders as her grip tightened. She could feel his heart pulse faintly against her ribs, could smell the salt on his collar and in his hair.

"Thank you." His hot breath filled the shell of her ear.

Heart stuttering painfully, Eliza could only nod and let his embrace keep her safe for a few moments longer.

Eleven

Eliza couldn't hide from her father any longer. She left the gallery early that day to meet him back in Torquay. One of Henry's drivers had picked her up, as promised.

When he wasn't trapped in his London office, Gerard Braybrooke spent his summers by the marina, polishing his yacht in his cargo shorts while the sun browned his skin. Eliza caught his bald head bobbing from the seafront right away and ambled down the docks slowly, nerves wracking her as she practiced her speech in her head for the tenth time that afternoon.

She had to do this. For Benny, and for all the people his art helped.

His yacht sat at the very end of the harbour, a dazzling, billowing white sail against the other rusting old boats and dingy masts. Gerard's stout frame swayed and buckled against the horizon as he shifted around the *Lady Eliza*. As though he sensed her presence, he peered over his shades and broke into a wide grin.

"Hello, princess. This is a surprise!"

Eliza forced a smile. "Hi, Dad."

He extended his hand and helped her aboard, pulling her into a sweaty, sunscreen-laced hug. The air had turned humid on this side of the coast, and Eliza had unbuttoned the collar of her shirt and freed herself of her blazer beneath the scorching sun. The seafront bustled with tourists, all of them dots on the sand from here. The kind of summer Eliza had loved as a kid.

"How are you, love?" Gerard pulled away and offered her a bottle of iced tea from the cooler. She accepted gratefully, planting her purse and blazer down as she rested against the railings. She was just about ready to dive into the sea herself, sweat trickling down her neck and dampening her back.

"I'm good. How are you?"

"Can't complain."

Eliza inhaled steadily. The rehearsed speech had already vanished from her head, but the anxiety drove her to begin anyway. "Dad, I've been meaning to talk to you about something. It's about Greystone."

"What's Greystone, love?" He swallowed a large gulp of beer, ruffling his shaved head as though forgetting no hair lay there anymore. It hadn't for at least a decade. "Don't think I've heard of it."

"The gallery." She fought back a roll of her eyes. Her father involved himself in so many businesses and causes, he had probably lost track. Though he was kind and loving, he became as cold as Henry when it came to work and money. Now that she had seen the other side of things — Benny's side — it only made her angry. "The one in St Agnes that you plan on co-owning with Mr. Weatherford."

"Ah, yes." Gerard clicked his fingers as it dawned on him. "That one. Henry tells me you're doing a wonderful job there."

It hadn't been what Henry had told *her*, but she didn't dare say so. "The problem is that Mr. Weatherford's son, Benny, has no idea he's about to be pushed out of his own place so that you can take over. Did you know about that?"

"What Henry does or doesn't tell his son is none of our business, love," Gerard chided.

"But I've seen how much he loves that gallery. To you, it's just another business venture. To him, it's everything — and it means a lot to the community, too."

Gerard scratched at his freshly shaven chin, eyebrows knitting together beneath the frame of his sunglasses. "It's not my problem, Eliza. Why are you bringing this up now?"

"I want you to back out of your deal with Henry," she said carefully, no longer a daughter, but a businessperson like her father. She was proud of the way her voice held, even as desperation and dread poured like ice into her gut. "You can run a million different galleries, Dad, but I don't think this one is for you. Benny doesn't deserve to have everything taken off him."

His features clouded, enough that she no longer felt the sun's warmth on her arms. "That boy is a mangey scoundrel who lives off his father's wealth without any show of gratitude. I shan't back out of a deal for his benefit."

"Dad," she pleaded, but was silenced a moment later by a dismissive wave of Gerard's hand.

"No, Eliza. I'm not sure where this is coming from, but you ought to be ashamed of yourself. The gallery will be a good investment, and I can guarantee I'll do a far better job at running it than Benjamin Weatherford. For you to suggest that I shouldn't go ahead with the deal is quite ridiculous."

Eliza shook her head helplessly, on the brink of tears. Nobody would listen to her, and Benny was going to lose everything because of it. "You have no idea what Benny is capable of. You have no idea what it means to him. You can invest in a thousand more galleries, but he can't. This is all he has, and you're going to take it away. Please, Dad. If not for him, then do it for me."

"I won't hear another word of this, Eliza." An anger Eliza had heard rarely in her childhood fringed his tone now, and he dropped his beer back into the cooler. The clatter was so loud that it made her jump. "My answer is no. If I can't trust you to do your job efficiently, I will hire someone who can. Is that understood?"

"Yes," she whispered hoarsely through the lump in her throat. She left the yacht without so much as a goodbye, trampling back down the docks with so much rage that the wood might have splintered beneath the spears of her high heels.

The hope might have left her, but determination did not. She would find another way to make sure Benny did not lose everything. She would do whatever it took.

She would not be the cause of his downfall.

Twelve

Eliza had managed to get some of Benny's pieces on display in the museum she had curated for in Exeter. It was the weekend of their annual arts and crafts fete, and with her connections, they had agreed to let Greystone Gallery be one of the sponsored businesses. They had spent the morning networking with other artists and gallery owners as children skipped in and out, faces and hands — and clothes — painted.

It was the most she had seen Benny smile in a while. He sat now on a miniature chair hunched over a miniature table, painting with a small group of kids who laughed hysterically at his terrible jokes. The sight awoke something in Eliza: something that left her tingling and full. She could only watch contently — until a little girl with her face painted as a pink, sparkly butterfly dragged her across the room, asking her to join in. Of course, she had to obey, kneeling as gracefully as she could beside Benny in her dress.

"Having fun?"

Benny grinned and tapped her nose with his paintbrush. "I am now."

Eliza gasped over the peals of laughter, searching for the stain. Her fingers came away yellow. "You laugh now, but I'll get my revenge. Just wait."

Benny's reply never came. His name echoed, high-pitched, around the gallery before it could, and Eliza turned to find a little blonde girl hurtling towards them, her grin daubed with something that looked an awful lot like strawberry jam.

"Uncle Benny!" she shrieked again, her arms flailing as she reached him. Benny had prepared himself into a crouch, and as she fell into his arms, he rose and twirled her around until her feet dangled through the air.

"Who are you?" he drew away from her to ask, blonde hair catching in his beard as her tiny hands pinched his cheeks. "Do I know you?"

"It's me, Uncle Benny! Pippa!"

"No, it can't be! My Pip is a tiny little baby." He nuzzled his head into her neck until she squealed — and then frowned when the sticky, red substance on her face caught in his hair. "Is that jam?"

"The mucky pup wanted a doughnut on the train," a woman sighed behind them. She had the same colouring as Benny, with smooth, straight brown hair and eyes the colour of rain-drenched soil. They sparked with the same warmth, too, though their smiles were entirely different. Benny's was crooked and charming: hers dimpled and loving — motherly.

Eliza felt as though she was interrupting something, and stumbled back on uncertain feet.

"I hoped you saved me one." Benny set Pippa down to hug the woman. "I'm glad you could come, Tessie."

Tessie. Eliza couldn't ever recall Benny mentioning a Pippa or a Tessie. And he *definitely* hadn't mentioned being an uncle before.

"Well, we were missing Uncle Benny, weren't we, Pip?"

Pippa was already finger-painting at the table and appeared not to have heard.

Benny's brows furrowed as he glanced back to Eliza — and remembered she was still standing there. "Sorry. Tess, this is Eliza. She's helping out with the gallery. Eliza, this is my sister, Teresa."

"Tess is fine." Teresa extended a hand and Eliza shook it, her grip weak against the bewilderment she felt.

"It's lovely to meet you. I, er... I had no idea that Benny had a sister." She'd been to visit the Weatherford's plenty of times as a child, and yet had never seen a girl there. She would probably have enjoyed her trips there a lot more if she had.

"Well, we have different mothers, and my father and I are... estranged."

Henry... Henry had a daughter, and Eliza had had no idea.

Was Declan the only one of his children he bothered to entertain? Teresa couldn't have been much older than her mid-twenties, though she had an air of maturity her brothers hadn't quite mastered yet. Why had Eliza never seen her before? Never known?

"Hey, Pip." Benny jiggled the little girl's shoulder lovingly. "Guess what?"

"Bag of snot!" Pippa burst into a fit of laughter that left everyone else chuckling, too.

"*Pippa!*" Teresa scolded with little commitment. "Don't be rude."

"I taught you well, kiddo." He held his hand out for a high-five that Pippa jumped to meet enthusiastically. "There's a planetarium upstairs where you can see all of the stars in the galaxy. How fun does that sound?"

Pippa's hazel eyes widened, and she stood clumsily from her chair. "Can we go?"

"Of course we can go." They began to wander through the gallery hand in hand, Benny pointing out his own photography before they ascended up the stairs. Eliza shuffled uncomfortably, feeling slightly lost — and perhaps slightly forgotten — until Benny turned on the first step and motioned over his shoulder for her to follow.

"Come on," Teresa grinned, "you've been summoned."

Eliza laughed and followed reluctantly, nodding towards the little girl skipping in front. "How old is she?"

Teresa rolled her eyes, the corner of her mouth sinking with a grin. "Six. God help me."

"She's adorable. I had no idea that Benny was an uncle."

"Well, Benny doesn't tend to share private details about himself where he can help it. I usually have to pry, bribe, or threaten just to find out how his week has been."

It sounded like Benny. Eliza was glad she wasn't the only one who felt Benny holding back — even if she had sat in on one of his art classes. She wondered if Teresa had been there when he'd been struggling, wondered how well she knew of her brother's problems.

As they began to climb the stairs, Teresa continued, "He's a good man, though. A good uncle. And he told me about you."

"He did?" Heat crept to Eliza's cheeks, body fluttering with the words. And that guilt, too, resurfaced from the cavern it lived in always between her ribs, reminding her of how terrible she was. How was still lying to him.

Teresa hummed. "You've made an impression."

Before Eliza could question her further, they stepped into the planetarium, into the comfort of the inky skies and glittering stars. Pippa had stopped in the heart of the dome, mouth agape and head tilted in wonder as she clutched Benny's hand. Eliza loitered around the side, the starlight passing over her face in orbs of silver. She could only imagine how it would feel being a child here, pulled suddenly into space.

Teresa crouched beside her daughter, and Benny rose, wandering over to Eliza before resting against the railings. "Sorry about that. I forgot to mention she was coming."

Eliza waved him off. "Don't be silly. It's lovely to meet them both. I had no idea you were such a family man."

"I try to keep Tess and Pippa separate from my father's world." And Eliza's world was his father's world, though it remained unsaid. But he had trusted her enough to invite them today. That must have counted for something.

"Why?" she couldn't help but ask, more bluntly than she'd intended. "If Henry's her father..."

"He doesn't claim to be. He doesn't want anything to do with her." His eyes darkened, voice lowering, until Eliza inched closer if only to show she was here, with him. His elbow brushed her side, and she wanted more. Wanted what he had given her that day on the beach last week. She had never felt closer to anybody than that day, and all they'd done was hugged.

"But why not?"

"Because she's proof. Tess isn't my mother's. And she was born before my mother passed away. She's proof of the fact that he cheated on his wife while she was dying."

Oh, God.

Declan had said that Benny had accused Henry of cheating. That that was one of the reasons their family had been cleaved apart, Benny excluded. He hadn't been trying to cause trouble. He had been telling the truth. "How did you find out about her?"

"Not long before I left the house for good, a woman I'd seen a few times in my dad's office turned up on the doorstep with a kid. My dad told me to go upstairs, but I didn't. I knew he'd been hiding something for years, but I never knew what.

"So I listened outside the door. I heard the woman, Teresa's mum, tell him that what he was giving her every month wasn't enough. She needed more money. And then when my dad refused, she threatened him. Told him she'd tell everyone about his affair. My dad paid her off and I never saw them at our house again. I couldn't forget, though. I had a sister, and I hadn't even known. It only clicked when I was older, when I saw the way he was with other women, too. God, I probably have a dozen siblings I don't know about. I found her details in my dad's office — old letters and cheques. Reached out when she was older, after I'd left. I couldn't do without her now."

The way he spoke of Teresa with so much tenderness... it was nothing like the way he spoke of Declan or Henry. Because his sister loved him. It was written all over her face. He loved her, too. They hadn't grown up together, but they'd chosen to build something better than Benny had ever had at home.

"Declan told me that you had problems because you accused Henry of cheating," she admitted. "Does he know about Tess?"

"He doesn't want to know." Benny's jaw squared in anger. "I've tried to tell him. I've shown him all the evidence I could find. But Dec is my dad's son through and through, and he'll never betray him as long as he has money and success. So they tell everyone I'm the family mess, and nobody has much trouble believing it. I suppose it's true. What else did he tell you?"

Her heart twinged. She had believed the worst in him so easily — and it was clear that he believed those things in himself, too, though he had no reason to.

"Nothing true," Eliza whispered finally, and laced her fingers through his. They stayed that way long after they left the gallery.

$$\infty\infty\infty$$

Benny hadn't expected Eliza to say yes when Pippa had asked her if she wanted to come to their picnic at the beach.

But she had—and he was glad for it. So was Pippa. His niece and Eliza had sung along to Disney songs all the way to Dawlish, and Benny had not been able to keep the joy, the warmth, he felt from splitting his face in two. Something had changed between them. She had learned his truth, his side of things, and had stayed.

It didn't stop the doubts, though. No matter what he felt for her, no matter how she made him laugh, made him feel new and untethered from the shadows of his past, she was still Eliza. She was still his father's employee. He couldn't forget that.

It was difficult not to when she skipped hand in hand with Pippa down onto the sand. Teresa lingered behind with Benny, a question glinting in her eyes, a bag of sandwiches and cakes rustling in her hands. "You seem very happy these days."

"Do I?" Benny tried to contain his traitorous grin; couldn't.

"Could your new lady friend perhaps have something to do with it?"

"My new 'lady friend' is my father's employee. Nothing more."

Teresa hummed, unconvinced. "Well, she seems to think a lot of you."

He hoped that the heat crawling up his neck could be passed off as sunburn. "I doubt it."

"You like her," she said bluntly, stopping him on the sand. Her brown hair whipped in lines across her face, and she attempted to tuck it back in vain. Though they only shared their father's blood, they were so alike in so many ways. More alike than Declan and Benny had ever been. "Don't do that Benny thing where you shrug it off and push her away. I think she's good for you."

Too good for him. Whatever strange tension had kindled between him and Eliza would fizzle out just as quickly. It always did. And someone like her, classy and elegant and wealthy, would surely never lower themselves to the exiled Weatherford brother. Not when she could have successful, wealthy Declan just as easily.

"She's seeing my brother," he confessed, though he no longer knew if it was the truth. Eliza hadn't mentioned Declan since that one date they'd had weeks back, and so much had happened since. Maybe he was just using it as an excuse; a reason not to trust her.

"Ugh." Teresa's face twisted in disdain. "Really?"

Benny shrugged, the shouts of his niece tearing his attention away.

"Mummy!"

"What, sweetheart?" Teresa asked.

"Can I go in the sea?"

Eliza and Pippa ambled back up the sand to them, Teresa crouching before her daughter with all of the motherly patience in the world. There wasn't anyone who Benny admired more than his sister. Pippa would never grow up the way that he did, rejected and alone. Though her father had lost custody of her after a long streak of incidents involving irresponsible parenting on his side, Pippa had all that she needed in just one woman, and Teresa worked every day to make it so. Benny wondered if he'd ever be a parent; if he'd ever feel that unconditional love for his own child.

Aware of Eliza's piercing gaze on him, he shook himself out of those thoughts and unfolded the picnic blanket that had been rolled in his hand. It wasn't actually a blanket, but a tartan scarf. He had forgotten to bring the mat he usually kept in his car for days like these.

He'd at least bought a bucket and spade for Pippa to build sandcastles, though it had been left abandoned in the sand as Teresa swapped her dress for a swimming costume and told her not to go too far in. Pippa tottered giddily down to the waves and began splashing.

"I miss being that age," Eliza said wistfully, pulling off her blazer and tying it around her waist. She wore a floral sundress beneath, a bow tied at her hip, and it left her curves more noticeable than ever. Benny had to force himself not to stare as he made himself comfortable on the blanket, stretching his legs out in front of him. It might have been easier if she wasn't so beautiful, all sunkissed and bright with the wind whispering through her hair, through the chiffon.

She sat beside him, careful to keep her legs crossed and her dress flattened against the breeze. Teresa had already followed Pippa down to the sea when she'd started splashing another child. Wherever she went, chaos followed.

"It was simpler then," he agreed finally, though it hadn't really been for him. His mother had been sick, his father distant when he'd been Pippa's age. At least then, he'd had his brother to lean on — but that hadn't lasted, either.

"Thank you for inviting me. It's been a long time since I last did something like this."

"Thank you for coming," he returned, gaze daring to lock on hers. She captured it, ensnaring him with those eyes the colour of the cloudless sky, and shuffled closer to him until her bare thighs, dimpled and pale, touched his. His breath hitched from the proximity. He imagined reaching out, pulling her closer still, imagined brushing back her hair and feeling those soft, pink lips on his.

He'd been staring. He looked away quickly, clearing his throat and squinting to find his family. They were still in the sea — Teresa too, now, the hem of her long dress getting tangled in the waves as she twirled Pippa around. He wished he'd brought his camera; but then was glad he hadn't. Sometimes, watching life through a lens only detached him from it, and he didn't want that today. He wanted to be here, with his family. With Eliza. If a day was all he got, he'd savour every moment of it.

"Want to go in?" she asked after a few moments of nothing but baking heat and words left unsaid.

Benny raised an eyebrow. "Do you?"

The same, glittering grin that Pippa wore when she was up

to no good laced Eliza's lips, and she stood, dusting the sand off her hands before offering them to Benny. "Why not?"

He couldn't think of a reason to give her, so he took her hands and stood, letting her lead him down to the frothing tide. Wary of the sudden cold, he hovered on the sand — but Eliza had other plans. She hauled him forward, giggling and skipping and splashing until he was lost in it, in her. His arms caged her without thinking as he drew her further in, no longer caring about his clothes, and she screamed and thrashed against him. Children again.

Benny couldn't remember a time he'd ever felt a joy like that before. All of the things that had been poisoning him for years slipped away in the sea. He was here, with a beautiful woman, being silly and chasing her through crashing waves, the taste of salt on his lips. Nothing else existed but that.

Nothing but a sudden cry close to him — a cry he knew. Tears streaked down Pippa's cheeks a few metres away. Teresa lifted her into her arms. With the churning ocean, he couldn't hear what had happened, but he waded over to them quickly, Eliza following behind with his shirt still bunched in her fingers.

"I cut my foot!" Pippa wailed. "Is it bleeding, Uncle Benny?"

"Oh no!" Benny gasped dramatically, peering at the wound at the corner of her toe. A bead of blood oozed from the small scratch. Nothing a plaster wouldn't fix. "It looks like it's going to fall off. Quick!"

He took Pippa from Teresa in a bundle of flailing limbs and rushed up the beach until she was bubbling with laughter again before setting her down on the blanket. The wind had already drawn the tasselled corner up, leaving sand scattered across it until the grains clung to everything.

"Is it really going to fall off?" Pippa's bottom lip wobbled as Benny searched for the dinosaur-patterned plasters he'd seen Teresa buy on the way here. He found them in the same bag as the box of cupcakes.

"Would I let that happen?" Cast in the looming shadows of Eliza and Teresa, he cleaned the cut with a bottle of water and fresh towel. "I'll give it a magic kiss, ready?"

His magic kiss was nothing more than a peck on Pippa's toe, but it still brought an unbridled, dimpled grin to her face.

"All better," he said proudly, bandaging the small scratch up with more plasters than necessary.

"Say thank you to Uncle Benny," Teresa said from behind him.

"Thank you, Uncle Benny." Pippa wiped her snotty nose on her arm and stood, the cut already long forgotten. "Can we look for starfishes, Mummy?"

He rose too, swiping the sand from his trousers. The damp denim chafed against his skin now, but he could not regret the few moments of bliss he'd had in the sea.

"Let's go then, monkey." They trailed away, Teresa flashing an appreciative glance over her shoulder as they headed towards the craggy cluster of rocks on the far side of the beach. He turned, blowing out a breath of relief — and froze.

Eliza was still looking at him, lips parted and eyes gleaming with an intensity that made him want to shrink and cower, as though she was scouring his heart, his soul.

"What?"

"Just…" Eliza shook her head, the ghost of a smile twitching at the corner of her mouth. "She's a very lucky little girl to have you as her uncle."

He was suddenly bashful. "I don't know about that."

"No, she is." Eliza inched closer, bare feet stepping onto the blanket and hands resting on his chest. "You keep surprising me. I was so wrong about you."

Warmth stirred in Benny's gut. Eliza's gaze flitted down to his lips, and he couldn't keep from drawing closer, from bowing his head. His fingers flexed with the urge to pull her to him, to have her soft curves fill his hands. He tested the waters; took another step toward her.

It was all she needed. Eliza burrowed into him, her nose brushing his as though asking for permission. He could feel her breath fan across his cupid bow, could feel her hands fist around his damp shirt.

And as much as he wanted, needed, he couldn't stop thinking about what it would mean. Eliza worked for his father. She was seeing his brother.

"We can't."

"Why?" Her breathy rasp left his stomach coiled and tight and desperate.

"My brother. You're…" In an effort to find himself again, to escape that overwhelming, all-consuming bubble of *her*, Benny took a step back and tugged at his knotted hair. "You're seeing my brother."

"No, I'm not. I haven't seen him since that one date, and I have no intention to."

Relief. Dread. Both of them eddied within him in equal measures. Because it was the only real excuse he could find, and he didn't trust himself to get it right. "It doesn't change anything."

Eliza's face fell. "Why?"

"Because…" He wrestled with himself, with his thoughts. A thousand of them swam around his mind, dizzying him until he couldn't breathe. "Because you work for my father. Because you and I aren't compatible in the slightest. Because this wouldn't just be a kiss for me, Eliza. I would want more. I would want everything, and I shouldn't."

"What if I want that, too?" A crease formed between her brows.

"You don't."

"How do you know?"

"Because you're you and I'm me." He sighed as though it was obvious. It was to him. He was all wrong, a rotten apple that had been chewed up and spat out, and she was… she was perfect. "I left your world a long time ago, Eliza, and I have no intention of going back."

He hadn't been prepared for the pain that crossed her features, the tears that glistened in her eyes. He couldn't understand them. He was doing her a favour. If they chased this silly little flame, his father would probably fire her on the spot. And God only knows what her parents would think. She wouldn't be able to bring him to those soirees his father held, or Christmas parties, or weddings. He wasn't like them. He wasn't respectable. He wasn't wealthy. He had driven himself free of that a lifetime ago, and there was no getting it back now.

"Right." Eliza nodded finally, voice cracking. "Fine. If that's what you want."

It wasn't. But somehow, that didn't seem to matter. It never had. So, he agreed silently and wandered off to the rockpools to find his family — even while his bones screamed at him to turn back, to tell her it didn't matter who they were, that he wanted her and didn't care about what anybody said.

But Benny had always been a coward. So he ran from her, from hope, from all of it, and prayed it would not chase him down again just to hurt him in the end all the same.

Thirteen

Eliza had never been more embarrassed. What had she been thinking, putting herself out there like that — with *Benny*? Benny, who had made his distaste for her lifestyle quite clear more than enough times before. Benny, whose father she worked for — *lied* for.

But she couldn't stop feeling that strange, electric cord tying them together, even when he had driven her home later that evening without a word. Perhaps she'd imagined all of it. She had always been the one to hug him or hold his hand. He hadn't shown any indication that he wanted her. And though she understood how complicated it was between them, a small, venomous little voice at the very cobwebbed corners of her mind wondered if it wasn't just their families that had made him push her away. Maybe it was her. Maybe he didn't like her, think of her, that way. A lot of men shied from her because of her body. He wouldn't be the first.

She knew that that part of her was only a pestering remnant of insecurity she had shaken off long ago. Because if Benny didn't like her that way, then she must have imagined the way he'd licked his lips hungrily at the sight of her sundress, the way his body had leaned into her when she'd inched closer to him.

Either way, she would let it go. What she wouldn't let go, though, was a way of solving the problem of the gallery being taken over, and a solution seemed to arise all by itself when she wandered along the seafront of Torquay on Sunday for some fresh air and found an empty property. Her mind immediately conjured up images of paintings hanging in the window. When she got home, she booked a viewing. Just to see.

That was how they ended up standing in the empty space

on Tuesday afternoon, sunlight pouring into a bright, airy space twice the size of Greystone. Things between them had been fraught, but she'd managed to convince Benny to come along, and he slouched in the centre of the room now, hands in his pockets and brows furrowed in confusion. "Why am I here again?"

"What do you think of it?" Eliza asked, dragging her finger along the sage green skirting boards.

"I think it's an empty building. What am I supposed to think of it?"

"You honestly can't imagine your work hanging in this place?"

"I already have a gallery," he said slowly, as though Eliza had suffered a blow to the head on the way here. "I'm confused."

Eliza sighed in exasperation. "Haven't you ever thought about expanding?"

"No," he admitted bluntly. "I can't think of much past trying to make enough profit to pay off my dad."

"What if you didn't have to pay him off?" she said. "What if you bought a new space for yourself, separate from him?"

He snorted his disbelief, scratching at the bristle on his chin. "Right. I can finally make use of that secret bank account I have with millions of pounds in it."

"You could get a loan," Eliza suggested.

"No bank would be stupid enough to loan me money."

She quietened at that, glancing around again. She couldn't stop imagining Benny here: drinking coffee behind the counter, painting in the backroom, holding classes in the smaller space through the arched threshold opposite. "Can't you see it, though? There's so much more space. Space for more classes and more work. There's an apartment upstairs, too."

"It's a lovely studio," he admitted, patting the white pillar in the centre as though it was an old pal. "But like I said, I'm broke. I'd never be able to do it."

"Well…" Eliza worried at her lip, hesitating, though some part of her already knew it was right. "I could loan you the money."

"Absolutely not." Features taut, he shook his head and

crossed his arms over his chest.

"Why? There'd be no rush to pay me back."

"I'm still paying off my debts to the last person I lent money from. At some point, I have to stop leaning on other people. Besides, why would you do that? What's in it for you?"

"Nothing." Nothing but the absolution of the constant guilt festering in her stomach. "I can just... I can feel you in here already, somehow. I don't know. It just feels like it should be yours."

Benny softened, his eyes flickering with warmth until Eliza was certain she was going to melt. He looked at her sometimes as though she was so much more than she was. As though he thought the world of her. She didn't deserve it. If he knew...

"I appreciate the thought," he said gruffly, shoe laces slapping across the lacquered floorboards as he wandered across the space again. "But it's just not feasible. Besides, the last thing I want is to relocate back here."

"Why do you hate Torquay so much?" she couldn't help but ask.

Benny only shrugged. "Bad memories."

Memories of losing his mother, perhaps. His father. His brother. She supposed she couldn't blame him for that. They had had very different childhoods here. "I understand, Benny. I do. But if you want to distance yourself from your father once and for all, I think it's going to take change. You should look into that loan. With a good proposal, you have a chance. Think about it. You don't have to buy this one, but there are hundreds of spaces out there that would be better with your work in them."

Benny made no promises, but the creases remained etched into his forehead all the way home, and Eliza knew. She had reached him.

∞ ∞ ∞

"I..." Benny seemed to struggle as though he'd lost the words on his tongue, pausing in front of the pile of marked canvases propped against the wall. His hands were caked in drying paint, his hair falling messily into his eyes as he bowed his chin to his chest. He hadn't looked at Eliza properly all day. Things were still uncomfortable with them, though they were both doing their best to ignore it. Still, Eliza had stayed late tonight for his support group again. She'd opted for watercolour this time, and had somehow found herself painting the sea and crags of Dawlish as it had looked on Saturday, gilded in sunshine, when everything had been better and easier. Before she had ruined it.

She continued to pile away the chairs now, unsure whether she would ever hear the end of his sentence — if there had been a sentence to begin with. But Benny still didn't move — not until he lifted his gaze finally, the intensity of it enough to draw Eliza's breath from her.

"I don't think I explained myself properly on Saturday."

A thousand nettles uprooted themselves in her gut, until her insides stung and burned. "You don't have to. It was a mistake. My fault completely."

"No, that's not true. We both…" Benny sighed and tugged at his hair, leaving specks of blue tangled in the knots. She fought the urge to reach out, to brush them away.

"It's okay," she said. "Really."

Frustration burned in his eyes and he shifted restlessly, as though there was something more he wanted to say. Eliza longed to know what it was — what he truly thought. Was she the only one who felt the constant, inescapable pull between them?

She wouldn't find out tonight. A shrill ring of a phone vibrated somewhere close. Benny cursed and dug into the pocket of his jeans, pulling out an old-fashioned, heavy-looking mobile and accepting the call. His brows furrowed as he did, lips pressing into a hard line that only tightened further as he listened to whoever was on the other end. Eliza knew she shouldn't try to eavesdrop — but concern had written itself all over his face, and then he was pacing as he murmured, "You're okay, mate. Where are you?"

She followed him back to the front of the gallery, where her painting and his still sat. She didn't even know what Benny had painted tonight. Hadn't dared ask in case he wanted to see hers. None of that seemed to matter now. Benny yanked his desk drawer open and pulled out his car keys, phone still pressed to his ear.

"I'm on my way. Hang in there, yeah? I'll be there soon."

Eliza's heart began to pound. His words were fragile, tender, and she worried it was his sister in some sort of trouble. He didn't seem to see her when he hung up the phone, already racing to the door.

"Benny?"

Benny swore in realisation, spinning on his heel. "Would you mind closing up for me?"

"Of course not," she frowned. "But what's wrong? Where are you going?"

Hesitantly, Benny chewed on his lip. "It's Glen. I'm his sponsor, and he's... He's relapsed."

The breath left Eliza in a sharp, ragged gust. Glen hadn't shown at the support group today, and though he hadn't said anything, she'd sensed Benny's worry at the fact. It made sense, now. "Can I come with you? Can I help?"

He shook his head, and she tried not to acknowledge the disappointment she felt. This wasn't about her. This was personal. Something Eliza couldn't possibly understand. Not the way Benny did. She wondered if he'd had a sponsor, a support group, a person to turn to when things were bad. "Glen wouldn't want anybody else to see him like this. I'm sorry."

"I understand," she whispered. "I'll close up here. Don't worry. Just... Let me know if there's anything else I can do."

Benny nodded, but he was no longer focused on her. He cast her the ghost of an appreciative smile before leaving, the gallery door slamming shut behind him.

In the quiet and the darkness, Eliza found her hands shaking, though she didn't know why. She barely knew Glen. It was more the pain that came whenever she thought of Benny enduring the same things. To distract herself, she wandered over to Benny's easel — and froze until she had to remind herself to breathe.

Like last week, Benny had strayed from his usual mono-
chromatic style with oil paints and vibrant colour. Only he hadn't
painted flowers this time. He'd painted a woman, blonde-haired
and saturated in dazzling joy as she splashed in a cerulean sea,
floral summer dress sticking to her curvy, dimpled thighs and
waist.

Her, she realised. He'd painted her.

Fourteen

Benny got home just before dawn, bone-tired and ready to collapse onto his sofa to save himself the extra steps to the bedroom. Glen had been in a bad place last night, and it had reminded him of all the nights he'd been unable to walk himself home or even remember his name. But he'd gotten Glen home to his wife and sobered, and then had stayed with him until he'd fallen asleep. Tomorrow, Glen's journey of recovery would start again. Benny still wondered how he'd found the strength to do it himself.

He tripped over his own feet on the way in, kicking off his shoes without caring where they landed.

And then he paused, unsure if exhaustion had left him prone to hallucinations. If it hadn't, then Eliza was sitting in his living room at five a.m., painting — in his shirt. In his state, he could only murmur a puzzled: "Huh?"

Eliza turned with her paintbrush suspended in midair, as though she hadn't heard him come in. She was smeared from head to toe in paint. Her hands, her arms, her face. Guilt flickered across her features, followed quickly by concern as she took him in. "Benny. Are you okay?"

"I am… confused," he admitted, scrubbing his hands across his face to wake himself up. Nothing changed. Eliza still stood in front of him, paint-stained, her blonde hair cascading down one shoulder and yesterday's make-up smudged beneath her eyes. "What are you doing here?"

"I was too worried to go home." She put the paintbrush down reluctantly, cleaning her hands on an old rag. "I sort of let myself into your apartment after I closed the gallery so I'd be here when you got back and… well. I needed a way to pass the time. Sorry. I overstepped. A lot."

"It's okay." And it was. He was glad not to come home to an empty apartment, no matter how badly he needed the sleep. He was glad to come home to her, looking a million times better in his shirt than he ever could. For a moment, he could pretend that this was his life. Their life. That they had kissed that day on the beach and hadn't looked back.

"What are you painting?" He made his way over, the corner of his mouth curling in delayed pleasure. The design was familiar — a lighthouse. The one on the headland overlooking the cliffs. The one he had taken a picture of. The original photograph had been pinned to the wall, black and white and full of shadows. Eliza had brought it to life with acrylic paints, capturing the red stripes and grey cliffs and sage-green grass. He could only gape at it in awe.

"Is Glen okay?"

"He will be," Benny answered absently.

"Are you?"

He looked at her, then — in surprise, in wonder, in whatever that constant fluttering of wings and claws in his chest was — and felt as though she had pierced right through him. As though she could see everything he felt without him having to tell her. "I will be. This painting is... It's wonderful, Eliza."

Eliza shrugged, barely sparing her work a glance. "It's been a long time since I could paint like this. I've missed it."

"Why don't you do it more often?"

"It always felt like a waste of time. Nothing will ever come from it."

"Does it have to?" He frowned. "Art for art's sake, right?"

Her eyes glazed in thought, a reply never coming. Blue paint peppered her nose, and Benny couldn't help but take the rag from her hands and dab it off. "You have paint on your face."

She laughed quietly, eyes fluttering shut against his touch.

And he couldn't help it anymore. He couldn't fight it. All of the reasons not to kiss her, not to feel what he felt for her, seemed to have drifted away. Rules and restraints seemed not to apply in the early hours of the morning. It was just them and the congealing paint and the singing birds outside his window, and he wanted it to be this peaceful, this right, always.

So he leaned in.

Eliza kept her eyes shut, breaths coming faster now as she tilted her chin to search for him. He didn't keep her waiting. His lips found hers as he dropped the rag and cupped the nape of her neck desperately. She gasped into him and deepened the kiss, fingers clawing at his shirt as though afraid he might pull away. He wouldn't. He couldn't. He was too tired to find a reason not to, even though he knew it would come back to him tomorrow.

Hands looping beneath her thighs, he hauled her closer, telling her he wanted — needed — more in the greediest of ways.

"I'm heavy," she whispered, and it almost broke his heart.

"You're perfect." It was the truth. She had waited for him to come home; worried about him; saved his gallery, his livelihood. And she wanted him. He didn't know why or how, but he could feel it almost as much as he could feel his own desires pressing against his skin. So, he urged her up, and she let him, legs resting on his hips as they stumbled together until she was braced against the wall. Her hands were rough with dried paint as she ran them across his flesh, leaving goosebumps in their wake. They found his neck, his collarbone, his chest, and unfastened the top buttons there.

Breathless and overwhelmed and alive, he drew away, his forehead resting against hers until she stopped; waited. "What's wrong?"

"Nothing." His voice was nothing more than a desperate rasp. And it was true. Nothing was wrong anymore. Because he had her. Because nothing had ever felt this way before.

So, Benny carried her to the bedroom, laid her down, and lost himself in her and all of the ways it felt so, completely right.

∞ ∞ ∞

Eliza woke up wrapped in him. Paint crusted every crease of her hands and knotted her hair, still. She picked at it absently while nestling into the warmth at her back. *His* warmth.

They had forgotten the day and slept until noon. Eliza did not ever want to leave his bed, leave him. As though sensing her thoughts, he pulled her closer still, fingers curling themselves into the softness at her waist and massaging the hinges of her hips. Her stomach curled at the memory of those fingers dancing across her body. He had taken his time with her, drinking her in as though she was a masterpiece. Eliza had never felt so beautiful, so right before, and so appreciated. He had been tender, careful, putting her needs first before they made love. Not once had he balked at her body. The opposite, really.

He had cherished every inch of her, and she could only offer the same in return. She twisted around now, wanting to see him. His brown eyes were hazy, lids heavy with sleep, but a tired smile curved beneath his beard as her fingertips waded through an invisible river winding along the side of his face, from his temple to his chin.

Benny hummed his pleasure, twining a leg between hers. "Hello."

"Hello."

"We should get up."

"Hmm," Eliza hummed her agreement — and yet neither of them moved. Benny's brown eyes stayed on her, darkening slightly. She pressed her thumb against his sudden pout as though she might be able to stop it. "What?"

"Nothing."

"Liar."

"It's just…" he sighed. "How is this going to work, Eliza? Do you even want it to, or is it just wishful thinking on my part?"

"How could you ask me that?" she frowned. "Of course I want it. I wouldn't be here, otherwise." She didn't sleep with people she didn't trust — not after she had learned that some men could be cruel and selfish and untrustworthy with her body. But Benny had never been those things. She'd trusted him completely, and he'd given her no reason not to.

Because it wasn't just the physical that had mattered. It was everything else, too. Everything they felt. Everything they were. It had never been that way before.

"Aren't you worried about our families? Your parents probably don't think very much of me. They probably wish you chose the other brother."

"I don't care what they think," she said, brushing her fingers through his hair gently. "That's their problem."

"Even with what you know about me." He swallowed, throat bobbing. "My past. I don't even have any money."

"You will when the gallery is finished." The lie came so quickly to her that it no longer felt like a lie at all. Because it wasn't. Because she would get him his gallery, whether it was here or somewhere else. "I'm not perfect, either. I don't care about your past or about money. Those things aren't who you are."

She could have sworn that his eyes glistened with tears. "Then we're doing this?"

Eliza sparked with excitement, and she kissed him on the nose lightly. "Yes. We're doing this."

They sank back beneath the covers together and explored one another as though it was the first time again — this time, with none of their wariness or fears holding them back.

Fifteen

Eliza had convinced her father to get to Henry's annual garden party early — even if his usual style *was* fashionably late. Nerves jittered through her, the knowledge that this was her last chance to persuade them from their plans weighed on her like a lump of cold steel. Benny would be here soon — his choice, "For the gallery's sake," he'd said last week when it had come up in conversation. She had to fix it all before he was, before his father told him everything.

"Mr Weatherford!" She found Henry in the grand, marble-topped kitchen sampling an array of canapés set out on silver platters in front of him. The caterer hovered sheepishly behind, but Eliza saved her from any criticism by pulling his attention away. "I'd like to talk to you for a moment, please."

Henry looked straight past Eliza to her father with a pleasant grin that, having once seemed friendly, now made her cringe. "Gerard. I'm glad you could make it."

"We haven't missed one yet, have we?" Gerard replied, shaking Henry's hand. "Sorry we're early. Eliza was a little bit eager."

"Not a problem. Can I offer you a drink?"

Eliza fought not to roll her eyes at the pleasantries — especially when Gerard accepted a tumbler of whisky and requested extra ice. A waitress fluttered around them as Henry led them both through to a parlour filled with far too many shades of white furniture. Eliza had never been allowed in here as a child, but she sat cross-legged on the couch now, her peach dress whispering around her ankles.

Henry sat in the armchair opposite, Gerard collapsing at her side. "It's the right weather for it tod —"

"I really *would* like to speak with you both before the guests arrive," Eliza interrupted. "I know that I've discussed with both of you before about how important Benny is for the gallery's image, and it hasn't deterred you from your plans of taking over, but I really must urge you to reconsider before it's too late."

"Eliza," Gerard grumbled, but she ignored him.

Instead, she pulled her tablet from her purse and swiped through a series of images of the gallery in its most recent stages of development. It was almost finished, inside and out, and tourists had been coming and going for weeks. She had made sure to capture them, too, as well as a spreadsheet of profits she had secretly copied over from Benny's old laptop. Henry glanced across every image with little interest, his lips pursed sourly as she spoke.

"As you can see, the gallery has quickly become a pillar of the St Agnes community and a hotspot for tourists, too. Benny has had more sales in the past week than he had the whole of last year. He's selling prints, postcards, art, and photography — and because the work is selling so fast, we're able to commission other artists so that the exhibitions are constantly in rotation. Benny has began offering more classes and we're thinking about workshops for kids —"

"Miss Braybrooke," Henry said calmly.

Eliza ignored him. "Benny has done everything you wanted. He's brought the gallery back to life. It would be so unfair, so cruel, to take that away from him now. We —"

"Miss Braybrooke," Henry repeated, scolding now.

She let her words ebb, finding herself breathless from her outburst. She had been talking like a madwoman. Heat sprinkled her cheeks at the realisation.

Gerard clawed at his collar, sweat beading down his sunburnt neck. "I'm terribly sorry, Henry. I have had words with her about this."

"As have I," nodded Henry. Eliza fought not to cower beneath his icy glare. "It seems she thinks too highly of my son. I can't imagine why."

Anger ground through her, metallic and hot. "With all due respect, you haven't seen the gallery in weeks. Why is it so difficult for you to see the good in your son, Mr. Weatherford? Why do you want so badly to tear him down?"

A flush of furious red blossomed across every leathery inch of Henry's face. He stood, placing his own glass down on the side table in a way she was sure many people found intimidating. Eliza did not startle. She kept her chin tilted, kept her eyes fixed on his with unwavering resolve.

"I have made my decision, Miss Braybrooke. You are walking on thin ice."

"I won't aid you in this," she said. "If you do this, I will take every piece of art I have curated in that gallery and find a new space for it. You'll have nothing."

"I *own* that art." Henry was one lip twitch away from baring his teeth. Her father remained silent — a submissive dog through and through. She despised them both for this. For everything they had made her do. "Are you forgetting whose pocket it all came from? Who funds the business?"

"It doesn't matter." Refusing to spend another moment in his shadow, she rose on determined legs. "Those artists are collaborating with Benny. With *us*. *We* secured their trust; promised them a safe place for their art. *We* chose them, built a partnership with them. Do you think they'll take kindly to a couple of businessmen who have never touched a paintbrush in their life coming in and turning the gallery into a place that's only there for people like you to spend thousands on pieces they'll never even understand or truly appreciate?"

"*Eliza*," Gerard scolded behind her.

But it didn't matter. Eliza could see that her words would never get through to Henry. She had meant what she'd said before: she'd find another space, another way. By the time she was done, Henry and her father would have nothing left but the bare skeleton of a building once meant for something more.

"Benny deserved a better father than you," she sneered finally. "So did Teresa."

Henry's face paled at the mention of his abandoned daughter's name. It brought Eliza little satisfaction now. If anything, she felt cheap for hitting so low. But these would be her last words to the cold-hearted man in front of her, and she wanted to hurt him the way he was about to hurt Benny.

So she left them lingering in the air as she pushed past him, into a flood of newly-arrived guests in the foyer.

Only then did she realise that she might just lose everything by the time the day was done. And then, she hoped that Benny didn't show up at all.

But he did — an hour and a half late, underdressed, and with a picked buttercup in his hand. He tucked it behind Eliza's ear, and she pretended as though everything inside her was not shattering while she still could.

∞ ∞ ∞

The first thing that Benny noticed was that his mother's wisteria plants — her pride and joy when he'd been growing up — had been left to shrivel and die, so that only a few overgrown smatterings of purple remained. The last pieces of her.

The second was that nobody would meet his eye save for Eliza. The faces around him were only vaguely familiar, more wrinkled versions of the awful people he'd been surrounded by during childhood. Even the maid was the same woman who had taken care of Benny as a child, though she seemed not to recognise him now as she walked past him with a platter of canapés.

He'd seen Declan in passing, ignoring him lest anybody see him reunited with the exiled Weatherford brother. Eliza was the only one who seemed not to care about what people thought. She led him into the marquee hand in hand, where her blonde-haired mother nursed a flute of champagne. She was so much like Eliza, though slimmer and paler and — he soon found — snootier. She turned her pointed nose up at him as soon as she caught sight of him.

"Eliza, dear. Would you like some salad?"

"No, thank you." Eliza's smile was strained, and Benny

squeezed her hand in reassurance. He didn't know why she was doing this. He hadn't expected her to. "Mother, I'd like you to meet Benny."

"I believe we've met before," she replied haughtily. "You were quite young then, I suppose."

"It's a pleasure to see you again, Mrs Braybrooke." Benny extended his hand. Mrs Braybrooke let it hang there with an un-impressed, sidelong glare and a sniff of discontent. As though she might catch something from his touch. He put it down, jaw clenching.

"I think I saw Declan by the pond, Eliza. How are things be-tween you both?"

"There are no things between us," Eliza answered.

"You went to dinner, did you not?"

She sighed, shuffling closer to Benny as though to prove a point. He wanted nothing more than to walk away from all of it now. He had done his time here. This part of his life should have been over.

But in giving into his feelings, in falling for Eliza, he had thrown himself back into the world he hated.

"Yes. Once. It went terribly."

"What did you order?"

"What?"

"From the restaurant," Miss Braybrooke elaborated with a subtle, elegant wave of her hand. "What did you eat?"

"What has that to do with it?"

Miss Braybrooke gave Eliza a pointed look that left Benny uncomfortable — and angry. What, exactly, was she implying? "You know a gentleman is wary of how a woman treats herself. Salad, for example, is more elegant and healthy than something heavy, like a steak."

He wanted to say something; opened his mouth to — but Eliza beat him to it. "Well, I had a full plate of nachos for starters. A big, fat, greasy burger for main. And a triple chocolate cheese-cake for dessert. I suppose we're doomed. Shame. Come on, Benny. I want to dance."

She tugged him away, and Benny was glad. His own fingers pinched at his sides in aggravation. He'd had no idea that Eliza's mother treated her that way, trying to police her diet as though it had any bearing on who she was. Perhaps they weren't so different when it came to families after all.

He hadn't expected Eliza to *actually* drag him to the tiles in the centre of the garden, where a few people swayed. A pianist jingled out an old, whimsical ballad in the corner, and as Eliza began to dance with him from side to side, he could close his eyes and pretend he was somewhere else where it was only the two of them. Despite his discomfort, he rested his chin against her hair, drinking her in any and every way he could. He could smell the lavender of her shampoo and the floral perfume. Her dress floated between them, low-cut and hugging her curves the way everything did. He could get used to this; to her. He could fall for her, drown in her, and it terrified him. And yet he wouldn't be here today without her. He wouldn't be able to face them if she was not so confident, so uncaring of everybody else's opinions.

She believed in him. Believed he was better than they made him out to be. It was more than he ever could have asked for.

"I had no idea it was like that with your mother," he whispered finally. He'd always assumed Eliza had been brought up in a house as warm and happy as she was.

"Being fat makes other people uncomfortable," she shrugged — and pressed a finger to his lips when he went to protest. "It's okay. It's not a dirty word. I'm fat."

"You're a lot of things, Eliza." He pressed a kiss to her forehead, letting his hands fall to the cushions of her waist. "A lot of wonderful, beautiful things. The way you look, your body, is just one of them."

A tender smile graced her coral-painted lips as she threw her hands around his neck and looked up at him. "Now you know how I feel about you when you bring up your past. It doesn't change anything for me. It doesn't scare me."

His chest warmed, and he was certain that it was impossible to feel this way. Good things didn't happen to him — especially not in the same austere house and gardens he grew up in. But here she was, dancing with him, giving him enough strength to get through the evening. Making him *feel.* Making him happy. He wished he could have told the him of five years ago that he would end up here, after a long recovery; that it would be worth it.

That he wasn't a hopeless case.

"Benny, there's something I need to tell you." The afternoon sunlight seemed to slip away all at once, a crease forming between her brows.

"What?"

She didn't have a chance to tell him. Their space, which had been so personal, so impenetrable, so *theirs,* was invaded, an arm drawing him away from Eliza. His father's arm. He stood with Eliza's father, now a balding, sunburnt man with too many laughter lines.

"Benjamin," Henry greeted. "You remember Mr. Braybrooke."

Benny swallowed down his pride to extend his hand once again. This time, it was at least accepted. "I do."

"Gerard," Mr. Braybrooke introduced with an oily smile. "Eliza here tells me that the gallery is doing well."

"Well, she's a brilliant curator," Benny agreed, and couldn't help but add: "And a brilliant artist."

Gerard wore all the pride of a smug parent — pride that Benny had never seen on Henry's face unless for Declan.

"Gerard is an avid art collector himself," Henry continued, guiding them all away from the slow dancers, to the empty, lily pad-infested pond. Eliza's hand had gone slack and clammy in his. Benny was surprised it hadn't slipped away as soon as they'd approached. "He approached me not too long ago with an offer of partnership — for your gallery."

Benny frowned. "I don't need a partner."

Henry let out a terse chuckle that told Benny he was the butt of the joke rather than a part of it. "The partnership would be between Gerard and I, Benjamin. It's time for a change, don't you think? Time for you to move onto your own endeavours with your own money."

A high-pitched roaring began to thrum in his ears. He was vaguely aware of dropping Eliza's hand; of her apologising; of Henry droning on about a change in ownership and image.

"What are you saying?" he interrupted halfway through Henry's sentence. "Are you kicking me out of Greystone?"

"Let's not be dramatic, Benjamin," Henry said. "I think this will be good for you. It's time to stand on your own two feet."

"But you hate the gallery. You hired Eliza — " *to make it better.* Not for him, he realised too late. For her father.

His gaze fell to her; the woman who he'd trusted. Admired. She had known. All along she had known that she hadn't been curating the gallery for him. She'd been preparing it for Gerard and Henry.

"You knew."

"I tried, Benny." Tears slipped down Eliza's rosy cheeks, as though *she* was the one who had been betrayed, lied to. "I tried to talk them out of it. I'm so, so sorry."

He couldn't even look at her. He snapped back to his father, to Gerard, hatred blazing in his eyes. "You can't take the gallery from me. I've spent years working on it. On commissioning artists, on finding hidden talent. It's mine. You can't."

"Only it's not your name on the papers, is it?" Henry cocked his head — never to be questioned in front of his friend. His new associate. "It's mine. I own every square inch of that place, and I can do with it what I wish. You're not qualified to be in the business."

"You told me that if I broke even, if I made a profit, you would hand it over to me." He jabbed his finger in accusation, anger seizing him. The other alternative was falling apart in front of him, and he wouldn't. Never again.

"I told you that the gallery would be yours when you could afford it." Henry sniffed, eyes darting around; making sure his beloved guests were not watching. "You will *never* be able to afford it, Benjamin. Now calm down. You're making a scene."

"What did you expect?" he bellowed. Eliza was at his back,

trying to pull him away by the arm, but he snatched it from her grasp. "You lied to me. You hired someone else to lie to me, too. You're taking everything from me!"

Not just the gallery, but Eliza. He had taken Eliza. Before Eliza had even been his to take.

He couldn't stay, couldn't face the weight of a hundred people staring at him as though he was the villain. He turned to leave, marching across the grass. Declan caught him by the arm halfway, a twisting, malicious grin twisting across his lips.

"I see you're still trying to be just like your little brother, taking my sloppy seconds." He nodded to something behind him, and Benny turned to find Eliza still standing there, face drenched with tears. "You won't get far with that one, though. She's a bit frigid."

Benny stopped seeing, stopped thinking, stopped breathing. His fingers curled so tightly into his palms that he was certain he would find blood there later. And then his hands were on his brother's shoulders, yanking on his shirt, and he was so close to hitting him —

Declan got there first, the two flying back down the garden and into somebody's legs as his fist smashed into Benny's face. A bone ground in his nose, bringing tears to his eyes. The crowd cleared a path as Benny crawled up, tasting bitter blood on his tongue. Declan laughed, his gelled hair unruffling into a messy heap.

Benny wouldn't miss his chance again. He pushed his brother back until Declan tottered over the piled rocks and his mother's old, moss-eaten garden gnomes, into the pond. Benny lingered just long enough to watch Declan sputter and thrash as though imitating the fishes; long enough to feel that satisfaction that meant nothing in comparison to the betrayal, the devastation, the white hot rage.

He turned to find three dozen different faces staring, wide-eyed — Eliza included, with her hands covering her mouth. She made to reach out for him. Benny left before she could touch him.

Another terrible memory to leave behind with his childhood home. He vowed when he reached his car never to return there again.

Sixteen

Eliza quit her job the moment Benny left, when Henry was still grappling to pull Declan out of the fish pond. She would never work for him or her own father again. She wanted nothing more to do with either of them, and she told them as much before racing through a crowd of bewildered and disgusted guests to find Benny.

He had already gone.

Heart drowning in the cold, thrashing waves of regret, she drove after him, back to St Agnes. But when she got there, after sitting through hours of Saturday evening traffic with nothing but her own self-loathing to keep her company, the gallery was empty and Benny's car was nowhere in sight.

Dread left her stomach plummeting through an unending abyss as she searched the streets, dialling his number over and over again until the eleven digits were burned permanently in her memory. She received no answer. She could think only the worst, could only imagine him falling apart. Would he relapse? She had no idea. They had never gotten far enough to learn those types of things about one another.

When her feet were blistered and bloody and her throat raw from crying, she could only go back to the gallery and sit on the doorstep, praying that Benny would come home.

But it wasn't his home anymore, she had to remind herself. Because of her, and because of their fathers. Where would he go when the place he loved had been taken away?

She found out long after the sky had darkened. Eliza was shivering, trying to cover her bare arms with her hands, when Benny's car rattled to a stop by the side of the gallery. Her throbbing legs almost buckled with relief at the sight of him climbing out of his car, bloody nose aside.

"Benny." It was all she could think to say. She should have thought about this, practiced something, while she'd been waiting, but she had been too worried, too guilty.

Benny barely glanced at her. His hair was mussed and tangled, his shirt collar askew, but he at least walked on feet that seemed steadier than hers felt as he pushed past her to unlock the door.

"Benny, please," she begged pathetically. "Let me explain."

He said nothing, and the silence only left her hollow — but he did not slam the door in her face. He left it open, left her the opportunity to follow in behind him. She took it without question.

"I didn't know until after you agreed to let me help you. When I found out, I did everything I could to convince your father and mine to change their minds. I swear, I did. I —" She paused, wondering if he was listening at all. He was too busy dismantling the exhibits, pulling artwork — his artwork, photographs, prints — from the walls and letting him clatter to the floor without care. "Stop. You'll ruin them."

He didn't stop. His movements only got angrier, until frames splintered and glass shattered.

"Benny," she begged, a sob building in her throat as she tried to pry his body away from the exhibits. "Benny, please. Stop."

"Why?" he erupted finally. When he turned to face her, Eliza wanted to shrink away. Tears stained his cheeks, pain — *agony* — haunting his eyes until they turned inky and unrecognisable. "They're not mine anymore. None of this is mine anymore. It never was, was it?"

"We'll find another place," she said. "This art is yours. These artists want to collaborate with *you*. Your father can't take that away."

Nostrils flaring and chin wobbling, Benny shook his head defiantly. "He can take everything away." And then his eyes flickered to hers for the first time since he'd come home, and she wanted to shrivel into nothing beneath the weight of accusation and heartbreak there. "So can you."

"No," she whispered — begged. "No. I promise you that we

will find another place —"

"There is no 'we', Eliza. You lied to me." He swallowed, something choked and mangled croaking in his throat. "Was it at least worth the money? Did he pay you extra to sleep with me, or was that just a way for you to pass the time in between the lying and scheming?"

Eliza recoiled at that, upper lip curling in disgust. That he could even *think* that of her… "It wasn't like that and you know it. What we have is real. What I feel for you… "

"I think you should leave." His raspy, cracked voice turned so hollow that Eliza's blood ran cold.

"No." She couldn't. Wouldn't. Her feet remained rooted to the spot, and she tried to reach out a hand —

Benny flinched as though it was a blade. She snatched it back, helpless and desperate. What had she done?

"I understand how it looks, Benny," she said, chin set in determination. "I understand that you've been betrayed by a man who's supposed to love you. I can't even begin to imagine how it must feel. But my heart is in this gallery just as much as yours is. I swear that's the truth. I intend to do everything I can to make this right. *Everything*. Because I don't care about your father — or mine. I don't care about the money. I quit as soon as you left, and every penny he paid me will be sent back. I'm sorry. I'm so, so sorry for lying to you. I thought I could convince them to stop this before I needed to tell you. I thought I could fix it."

He was back to not looking at her. His fingers curled at his sides, chest rising and falling in heavy heaves — lost somewhere she couldn't reach. "Please go, Eliza."

"Just don't tear the place apart," she begged, backing away. If she pushed him any further, she'd never get him back. "We'll find a home for it. I promise, we will."

Benny didn't reply — didn't even appear to have heard her. So Eliza only took one last, painful glance through the gallery. The places they had bickered and the places that had been made new and alive again. His photography and her painting of Greystone. The space in its heart where he'd held support group sessions, where Eliza had realised he was a better man than any other she'd met before. The stairs leading to his apartment, where they had kissed and made love for the first time.

She had played a part in all of this being ripped away. But she would get it back. She vowed that to Greystone and to Benny as she left the gallery, numb and ruined and lost.

She would get him back.

∞ ∞ ∞

It turned out that, after a week of crashing on Jim's couch and living off Pot Noodles, the bank was stupid enough to grant Benny a loan. A small one, but with Jim's help with the proposal, it was enough to at least find a small property somewhere.

He hadn't been back to the gallery since the day after he had found out. He didn't want to see his father and Gerard tear down everything he'd built. He didn't want to see Eliza, either. Not until he'd cleared his head.

Though he hated the thought of moving back to Torquay, he'd queried about the studio Eliza had taken him to anyway — just to see. He needed to find a place as soon as possible, so that he at least had a chance at finding a place for the artists he'd already collaborated with — before Henry burned it or put it all in gilded cages. But the property had been sold. A blessing and a curse.

And then Eliza texted him an address the following day. The gallery they'd visited in St Ives, owned by the pretentious, linen-wearing Dean Scott, who hadn't approved of Benny's grey-scale style. He wasn't going to go. Not until Jim peered over his shoulder and shoved him out of the door. Benny had shouted through the letterbox to remind his friend that he was still wearing his striped pyjamas.

That was how he found himself standing uncertainly in the middle of Coral Reef Art and Photography now, unshakeable curiosity lying heavy in his gut.

He wanted to hate Eliza. He wanted to push her away, forget

about her. But he'd seen the pain in her eyes that night. He'd seen the guilt. And he couldn't stop missing her, always. He'd kept the lighthouse painting in the boot of his car, the only belonging that remained, save for clothes and paints. Besides he was in the area anyway to look at another property nearby. That was how he justified his own weakness as he tread on uncertain feet into Coral Reef Art and Photography — and found that it had changed completely from how he remembered it.

There were no bland landscapes on display now. No, it was *his* artwork, his friends' artwork, that hung on the white walls. It was almost as though he had walked into Greystone again, only the space was too big, too open, too new, and the acrid stench of fresh paint made him dizzy.

The clicking of heels against floorboards drew his focus away from all of that — to Eliza. She stood nervously behind the counter, hands clasped in front of her and a sheepish grin on her face. "Surprise."

Surprise was an understatement. Benny couldn't keep from gawping, brows knitting together in confusion. And beneath that, his heart racketed as it always did at the sight of her — another traitorous muscle he had not been able to train even after betrayal and time apart. "What is this?"

"I believe it's an art gallery." An echo of the words he had taunted her with the first day she'd walked into Greystone, all stiff-spined and professional and yet still so ridiculously, infuriatingly beautiful.

"Why is my art in it?"

"Because it's yours," she said. "If you want it, that is."

"What happened to Mr. Dean?"

Eliza shrugged. "Apparently he wasn't doing as well with this place as he let on. He had to sell it. Imagine how happy he was when I was the one to turn up and take it off his hands."

His eyes widened. "You bought it?"

"Presumptuous of me, maybe, but yes. I told you that I would fix this, Benny. I was never going to leave you high and dry."

Benny sucked in a jagged breath, pacing around to scan

every corner, every inch. She had bought it for him. It was his if he wanted it. His pride rose then, a sharp lump that left him cold. "I can't accept it."

"Why not?"

"Because I'm not a charity case. I've learned my lesson from accepting help or investments or whatever you're trying to pass this off as."

Pain, regret, twisted across her features. "I'm not trying to pass it off as anything. I'm not your father, Benny. This isn't a bribe or charity. It's a gift. It's a repayment. You reminded me of how important art is in all of its forms and all of its ways. It's only right that I show you how much that meant to me."

He couldn't. Not like this. Not after the lies and the hurt. "I can't. I'm sorry." He made to leave, but her voice, strained and thick with tears, brought him back.

"I had already put an offer on the place before the garden party, just in case. I thought you should know that."

He turned with some reluctance, chest clenching at what he found. She seemed so small standing behind the counter, soft, watery features swimming in pleas.

"It doesn't make it right. I know that. Nothing I do will ever make it right. But you have to know that I was always on your side. Your art needs a home. Here seems as good a place as any."

"And what about you?" he asked. "What will you do?"

A glimmer of a smile, solemn and heart-wrenching enough that he wanted to kiss every inch of it. Even now, he couldn't stop feeling. Wanting. Loving. He didn't trust easily, and yet he had with her. He still wanted to, even after she had breached that. Because a part of him knew that Eliza had been telling the truth when she'd said she'd tried to talk Henry out of it. He knew that there was only goodness in her, even when she was fierce and argumentative, and she would never have hurt him on purpose.

This, here, now, only proved it.

"It looks like you need a new curator," she shrugged.

Benny couldn't reply to that. Not yet. Instead, he turned his attention back to the art. There wasn't one piece missing from the collection he'd had at the gallery. "How did you get them back from my father?"

"When I contacted the artists about what had happened, they refused to have their work associated with the new management. They believed in you too much, Benny. They wanted to collaborate with *you*. I told them my plans to relocate, and they agreed without question." This time, he couldn't help the disbelief that rumbled from his chest. "Henry and Gerard are currently running an empty gallery. There's nothing left from there."

He had no doubt that they'd find something, some way of making money and profiting off naive tourists — but it wasn't his problem. His work was here, safe. So was Eliza.

"So, what?" Benny slid his hands into the pockets of his jeans awkwardly, scuffing the toe of his shoes against the lacquered wood. "We just take over this place and live happily ever after?"

"Can't we?" Her blue eyes glistened with the same hope that crushed him.

He wanted to. He could see it; could see them. Collaborating with artists. Holding therapy classes and summer fetes and workshops for kids. He could see Pippa running around with paint-covered hands, and he could see Eliza hauling in new pieces of work every week with a proud grin on her face.

He could see it all. But it wasn't that easy.

Was it?

"I, er… " he raked his hand through his hair, "I took out a loan. Turns out I could do that after all."

Eliza let out a laugh that Benny wished would last longer. Forever. "Well, a wise woman did try to tell you. I'm proud of you. Really. I think this could really take off for you."

He was trembling now, and though he hated to admit it, he had made his decision before he'd even walked through the door. This place was his. His artwork was at home here. *He* was at home here. He didn't know if it was the gallery or Eliza that made it so. He only knew one could not exist without the other. "Excuse me a minute."

Eliza frowned, but Benny wandered out of the gallery without a word, heading back to his car. He returned a minute later with a canvas in his hand. Eliza's lighthouse.

She'd had her back to him, but she whipped around when the bell above the door tinkled — and everything in her turned to sunlight as she took in the painting he held. He knew, then, that she deserved a second chance; that he could trust her completely; that he loved her and would stupidly, hopelessly try to make her smile that brightly every day he could.

"What do you think of 'The Lighthouse' as a name for this place?"

"I think it's perfect."

"Good." He placed the painting down, ready to be hung in the window — where it belonged. "Because it's yours, too."

"What do you mean?" She approached carefully, as though afraid one wrong move might send him running again. But Benny was going nowhere, and he made to meet her in the middle, lacing his hands through hers.

"I mean," he breathed slowly, "that it's ours. You made me believe in my art again, Eliza. I couldn't do any of this without you here."

"You want to run it together?" Her free hand crept to his nape, fingers tangling in his hair. He had missed that touch, and his eyes fluttered shut momentarily. The peace she brought him was not something he'd ever expected.

"Yes."

Tears shone on her cheeks as she nodded. "Then yes. If you want me here, I'll be here. Always."

And he would want her here always, too, though he couldn't find the courage to say so yet. That would come later. They had time, and he had no intention of wasting any of it holding back from her. For now, he bowed his head, meeting her lips halfway in a soft, salt-laced kiss that left him trembling. He gripped onto her as though she was a lifeboat in the middle of the choppy sea, and he didn't let go; wouldn't let go.

"I want you here," he vowed. "Always."

Epilogue

The Lighthouse had flooded with more sunshine than Eliza had ever known. Most of it seemed to radiate from Benny. The rest, the visitors stepping foot into the brand new gallery for the first time.

After a month of planning and redecorating and networking with more local artists, they had opened their doors to St Ives for the first time on a brilliant, late-summer's day — and the turnout had been more than either of them had hoped. Eliza's own painting of the lighthouse beaming out onto the sea had been displayed in the window, the gallery's trademark, never to be sold. Beside it, Benny's buttercups. He even had a few other pieces scattered around, as did she. They had braved putting themselves out there together — and she had been reminded of how art was supposed to be: messy and from the heart.

"Uncle Benny!" The screeching little girl pushing through the crowds could be none other than Pippa. She hurtled into her uncle's arms without care or warning, laughing giddily when Benny whirled her around as he always did. "Aunty Eliza!"

Eliza's chest warmed when Pippa fought to get down to tumble into Eliza's arms instead. "Hello, you."

Teresa was not far behind, drawing her brother into a hug before she did the same with Eliza. Though she and Benny had been together only a short amount of time, Eliza already felt part of their little family — a good thing, since she had finally distanced herself from her own. Both her mother and father had tried to reach out, but she needed space and time from them. She needed this, here, now: love and art and happiness. The bad things could wait.

Once she'd caught up with Pippa and Teresa, she spent her time handing out pamphlets advertising Benny's free art therapy groups and answering queries from visitors — and felt more at home than she ever had at an exhibit before. Because this one was personal. This one was hers. Theirs. She hadn't just curated it. She'd built it from the ground up, and she'd done it with somebody she loved.

Arms snaked around her as she admired one of Benny's photographs for a moment — still black and white, but lighter, somehow. Free of the shadows that had hung over his head for so long. It was her. A portrait he had taken on a lazy Sunday, sunlight streaming through the apartment they now shared in sharp slices that left her pale eyes translucent and her lips dark.

"Like what you see?"

Eliza turned in his arms, resting her hands against his chest and smiling without any attempt at restraint. "I do now."

Benny snuck a delicate kiss on the tip of her nose, every bit of him glistening with pride. For himself, and for her. She didn't think anybody had been so proud to be hers before. "Me too."

She realised only when her fingers trailed through something damp that Benny's shirt had a yellow handprint on it, and the wet paint had transferred onto her skin.

"Pippa," he explained with a low, rumbling chuckle.

"Don't let her touch the walls."

"I don't know. You can never have too much colour." He tore away from Eliza to admire the gallery, white-walled and sleek as it was. For how long, Eliza wouldn't dare guess.

"Then don't let her touch the art," she laughed, catching a glimpse of the little girl squirting paint at another child — and Teresa scolding her a moment later before apologising to the mother. A little terror, but impossible to be angry at for too long. Pippa could tear the place to shreds, and Eliza would still have all of the time in the world for her new niece.

When she looked back to Benny, she found that he wasn't looking at Pippa at all, but at her, his brown eyes swimming with something that burrowed straight into her heart, her soul.

"What?"

"Just... Thank you," he said quietly, emotion fraying his

voice.

"For what?"

"For believing in me."

Eliza softened, tracing a paint-stained finger across his bristly jaw, to his lips. "Thank you for believing in me."

He leaned in for another brief kiss — but Eliza stopped him, narrowing her eyes on the familiar face behind him.

Henry Weatherford stood in the middle of the gallery, wreathed by his son's art; the art he had tried to take away. Hot, defensive anger rose in Eliza, but Benny kept her grounded with his hand around her waist.

"It's okay," he murmured calmly in his ear. "I invited him."

She frowned, but Benny was no longer focused on her at all. The colour drained from his face, throat bobbing as he nodded at his father carefully: a warrior ready to face his battle.

"Glad you could make it."

Henry scoured the space with a haughty nonchalance, wincing when one of the children screeched nearby, loud enough to pierce through the walls. "I was surprised to receive your invitation."

Benny shrugged. "I wanted you to see it for yourself."

A tug at the frills of her skirt ripped Eliza's attention away from the conversation. Pippa stood at her legs, wide-eyed and oblivious.

Henry's granddaughter.

"Can you paint my face, Aunty Eliza?"

"Well," she hesitated, unsure of how to handle this foreign territory. As far as she knew, Henry had never even stepped into the same room as Pippa before. "Maybe in a little while. Where's your mummy?"

Pippa pointed to the corner of the gallery, where Teresa had frozen, face wan at the sight of her father. Eliza could only imagine what it felt like to see him after all these years.

"Pip," Teresa ordered, weaving through the crowds and extending her hand. "Come away. Uncle Benny and Aunty Eliza are busy now."

"It's fine," Benny said, taking Pippa's other hand. "This is my sister and my niece, father. Teresa and Pippa."

Henry's face grew slack, cold eyes flitting between his daughter and granddaughter. All of the people he had abandoned and neglected in one room. If Eliza didn't know any better, she would have sworn something softened in him.

Any weakness in him dissipated as soon as it came. Henry sniffed and straightened his spine again, though a traitorous muscle still quivered in his jaw. "I suppose you're feeling rather smug, now."

"Smug?" Benny cocked his head. "No. Proud of myself, of what I've accomplished? Absolutely."

His father only nodded, glancing around a final time. He didn't so much as skim over Teresa and Pippa again. It made Eliza nauseous, but she played with Pippa's ash-blonde braids and reminded herself that they were better off without him. They all were.

"How does Greystone fair?"

"Well enough." There was none of Henry's usual conceit in his voice, and that told Eliza enough.

"Good." Benny inclined his head once, politely. "Enjoy the exhibit."

Henry did not stay long enough to. He swallowed, glancing at Pippa just once before marching straight back out of the gallery.

"Who was that man, Uncle Benny?" Pippa asked.

"That was my father," he said, gaze filled with apology when he looked to his sister. "I didn't think he'd come, Tessie. I'm sorry. I should have warned you."

"It's okay." The lines at the corners of Teresa's mouth sank with a forced smile, but she pulled her brother in for a hug all the same. "I'm proud of you."

So was Eliza. So proud that she could burst. Still, as Teresa dragged Pippa back to the children's painting area, she looked at him in question, waiting for an explanation. Henry's appearance had not only surprised Teresa.

"I wanted him to see that I was better off without him,"

he admitted timidly. "I know he doesn't care. He never will. But I wanted him to see it anyway. I truly didn't think he'd come."

"I'm glad he did." Eliza pulled him close, her hand rubbing soothing circles across the faint knots of his spine. "I hope he saw just how much he's lost."

"And just how much I've gained," he murmured into her hair, dipping his head back slightly to look at her. "I've never been this happy before. I love you, Eliza. Maybe it's too soon to say that, but I—"

"I love you, too." The words fell from her without warning. For weeks, they had been fluttering just beneath the surface of her, like butterflies waiting to be freed. She meant them. She loved him more than she had ever loved anybody, and everyday, she found new reasons why.

The world fell away when he kissed her: the crowds and floorboards and the art. But it lived in them, still, painting their hearts and souls the same colour until Eliza couldn't tell where his ended and hers began.

She would never paint over it, not as long as he held her this way, loved her this way. They were made from the same brushstrokes, and Eliza trusted each stained, rough bristle of him completely.

Acknowledgement

I want to thank Ivy and Leah, first and foremost, for believing in my words and worlds even when I didn't dare to. The writing process would not be nearly as enjoyable if I didn't have the both of you to scream about my characters with and pathetically cry to when moments of doubt hit.

To my family, who nod and smile when required and have supported me through years of blood, sweat, and tears. And to Enzo the dog, who interrupted me midway through writing this to sit on my lap.

To you, reader (on the off chance I have one). Paint the world with your colours. It's brighter with you here.

About The Author

Rachel Bowdler

Rachel Bowdler is a freelance writer, editor, and sometimes photographer from the UK. She spends most of her time away with the faeries. When she is not putting off writing by scrolling through Twitter and binge-watching sitcoms, you can find her walking her dog, painting, and passionately crying about her favorite fictional characters. You can find her on Twitter and Instagram @rach_bowdler.

Books By This Author

The Divide

The Flower Shop On Prinsengracht

The Fate Of Us

Saving The Star

Dance With Me

Along For The Ride

Holding On To Bluebell Lodge

No Love Lost

The Secret Weapon

Printed in Great Britain
by Amazon